AGNARR'S JARLIN
ABANDONED ON NIFLHEIM

JENIFER WOOD

AGNARR'S JARLIN
ABANDONED ON NIFLHEIM
BOOK TWO

JENIFER WOOD

Copyright © 2023 by Jenifer Wood

All rights reserved.

No part of this book may be reproduced in any form or by any electronic or mechanical means, including information storage and retrieval systems, without written permission from the author, except for the use of brief quotations in a book review.

This novel is entirely a work of fiction. The names, characters, and incidents portrayed in it are the work of the author's imagination or have been used fictitiously and are not to be construed as real. Any resemblance to actual persons, living or dead, events or localities is entirely coincidental.

Jenifer Wood asserts the moral right to be identified as the author of this work.

Copy editing: Samantha Swart

Cover art: Rowan Woodcock

Cover design: Ash Raven

ISBN: 979-8-9879953-2-7 [Ebook]

ISBN: 979-8-9879953-3-4 [Paperback]

❦ Created with Vellum

*For my fellow anxiety sufferers, who get up,
and fight the battle every single day.*

A NOTE ABOUT CONTENT

I am a lazy reader and used to never read the content warnings. And then I realized I am also an *anxious* reader and would love a heads-up if things are about to get dark. This series is relatively light but I want to be sensitive to all readers. So, you can view this as a content warning, or you can view this as a menu.

Either way, *spoilers ahead.*

- Alien Abduction
- Anxiety/Mental Illness
- Mentioned parental neglect
- Explicit sexual scenes
- Hair pulling (consensual)
- Rough sex (consensual)
- Knotting
- Stretching and stuffing
- Misogyny
- Prejudice against humans
- On page violence (minor)

A NOTE ABOUT CONTENT

Mentioned

These are warnings for content that is mentioned, generally in the past, and in reference to a secondary character.

- Domestic violence
- Self-harm
- Neglectful/absent parents
- Military Sexual Trauma
- CPTSD/PTSD
- Depression
- Sexual assault
- Death of parents
- Chronic illness

CHAPTER 1

PIPER

I sighed into Agnarr's chest. It felt as if we had been riding Sindri all day. I was anxious to get back to the tribe but I was also exhausted. Between the trip to Snaerfírar and the mating frenzy, I was exhausted. I didn't know if I wanted to nap or get on my knees and suck Agnarr's cock. Maybe both? The mating frenzy was no joke. It felt as if Agnarr and I had fucked everywhere and in every way possible in the caverns, but I was still ravenous for him, exhausted as I was. My head lolled to the side against his chest as I attempted to stay awake.

"Not much further, Pip, just hang on," Agnarr whispered, urging Sindri along.

"Is there going to be some sort of celebration something or other we will be expected to attend when we arrive?" I asked. "I don't think I have it in me physically or mentally."

"No, if we arrive after dark, we can slip into my room and have everyone discover us in the morning. I would, however, recommend sleeping well tonight. Tomorrow will be full of celebration. A new Elska mating, a new jarl and jarlin? We will likely celebrate for weeks," he said quietly.

"Okay. I can do that. No blow jobs tonight," I said, words slurred, practically asleep.

"Pip, I would never expect that," he replied, voice strained.

I stifled a laugh, Agnarr was still getting used to enthusiastic blow jobs.

We were so close to the village that I could see the arch that welcomed us within its borders. Agnarr was right. The lights were out, we'd be able to slip in unnoticed. He nudged Sindri on, to the room I'd spent my first few days in. I hadn't noticed before, but there was a hitching post outside. He dismounted and tied her to it before lifting me off the saddle. He carried me bridal style over the threshold of his room and into his bed.

"Strip," he said simply.

"Wha—what?" I stuttered.

"We are mates. There will be no clothes between us. Especially not those dusty and worn from travel," he responded.

I'd never slept naked with a partner before. Heck, due to shared rooms as a child, I had never slept naked at all. But I was exhausted and Agnarr was peeling off his clothes while keeping his eyes on me. I toed off my boots, then removed my leggings and tunic.

"I am going to need more warmth if you expect me to sleep naked," I said as a chill ran up my spine, the lack of warmth noticeable with the unlit fireplace.

But it was like Agnarr could read my mind, already working the tinder and flint to set the logs aflame. It wasn't long before the glow filled the room, accompanied by the merry hisses and pops of the logs.

"Now, to bed. I don't want my mate exhausted when I introduce her to my tribe," he said gruffly.

I climbed into bed awkwardly. But Agnarr joined me immediately, his warm body engulfing mine.

"Um, how am I supposed to get any sleep with your hard cock pressing into my ass?" I asked.

"You'll ignore it, the same way I have to," he said, seemingly unbothered.

I settled in, using his bicep as a pillow. I wanted to lay him on his back and suck his cock until he came all over my chest, but we were both tired.

"Maybe we could do something about it in the morning?" I said, hopefully.

"Já, if we rise early enough, we may have some time together," he whispered, nuzzling my temple.

I tried to ignore his cock prodding into my ass. I wanted it, but I wanted to sleep more. I snuggled into his chest, trying to ignore our nakedness. I remembered I had tried to sleep naked once. It hadn't gone well. Noah and I had dated after college and it had gotten to the point where I had a toothbrush and pajamas at his house. He said he felt sleeping in the nude was "inappropriate" even though we were having sex regularly. I rolled my eyes. I was so done with being repressed by men who didn't understand me—or my trauma.

Agnarr's breathing evened out, suggesting he'd fallen asleep. So I did what I could to stop the mental spiraling and just enjoyed his embrace. It wasn't long after that I drifted off as well.

AGNARR

I woke up in my room, comforted by the familiar surroundings. The fire had burned down low in the night, but the room was still warm. What I wasn't used to was the tiny creature plastered to my side. I was on my back and Piper was wrapped around me, both arms and legs clinging to me. She snored softly in her sleep, peacefully unaware that I'd awoken. Looking out the window, it was just barely dawn. I wanted to let her sleep as long as possible. I was afraid to breathe, in fear of waking her. I stroked her hair, admiring her as she clung to me, trying to remain as still as possible. Her mouth hung open, while the sunlight lit up the highlights in her vahlnut hair.

I still couldn't believe she was mine. *Forever.* We had the Emarks to prove it. She'd accepted our bond. Elska mates. I thought of her growing ripe with our young, and my cock grew impossibly hard. I had always wanted orklings, but the idea of Piper carrying them was almost more than I could manage. Her thigh was resting on my cock and I tried to move away without waking her, the pressure being almost unbearable. I shifted and Piper tugged me closer to her. Her eyes fluttered open.

"Good morning," she said, sleepily.

"Hi," I responded, voice husky.

"Oh, have you been awake for a while?" she asked.

"Just a few moments."

"Well if the pressure I feel on my thigh is any indicator, you are in need of some relief."

Her hair was mussed, and she was barely awake but she trailed kisses down my chest directly to my hard cock.

"You should have woken me up," she purred.

"Um...this isn't something I am used to," I said hesitantly. I had been with many of the female orcs of our tribe, but spending the night together in my bed was new to me. I'd insisted we sleep naked because I wanted to stroke her soft skin as we slept, but I was just as new to matehood as she was.

"Well, it's something I will more than happily provide. Do

you want my mouth or my pussy?" she asked, grinning up at me.

Gods. I didn't know what to do with this female. *Pussy or mouth? Uhhh...*

"Pussy, if you're willing," I replied, trying to keep the strain out of my voice.

She pushed me flat on my back and swung herself over me.

"You may need to get me a little wet and ready, but pussy is definitely an option," she breathed.

I could feel her heat pressing against me and I groaned at the sensation. I pulled her in for a rough kiss, my tongue invading her mouth. She moaned, wrapping her legs more tightly around my waist. I was never more grateful that I'd insisted we sleep naked. I dragged my hard cock along her already damp core. The scent of her arousal was heavy in my room, driving me insane with lust. She continued to kiss me while grinding against me with her hips.

"Are you wet enough to take me?" I asked, breathlessly.

Piper breathed in deep through her nose, before reaching down between us to notch my cock at her entrance.

"Yes. Please. Need you inside me now."

She shifted, lowering herself on slowly my cockhead, causing us to both groan in pleasure. She circled her hips to work her way down, even with the amount of sex we'd had, our size difference was still readily evident.

"Is this alright? Is it too much?" I stroked a thumb across her jaw.

"It's good," Pip breathed—strained—focusing on continuing to take as much of me as she could. "I don't know how we are going to become jarl and jarlin if all I want to do is stay in bed a fuck you," she said as she slipped all the way down past my knot.

She placed her hands on my chest and took a breath. I

didn't thrust, wanting to give herself a moment to adjust to my size. It took me a moment to realize she was waiting for a response to her concern.

"The tribe will be patient. They know the mating frenzy. We will be given space," I pulled her to me for a kiss, "Astrid knew I wouldn't be ready to take on jarl the moment I found my Elska mate."

Piper leaned back and slid almost all the way off me before slamming down, impaling herself again and again.

"Is this how it will always be?" she panted.

"What do you mean?"

"I've never—*never* had sex like this. Just the thought of your cock inside me has me ready to come," she responded breathlessly.

"Well, you can't have had very good sex before this," I said, thrusting up, grinding myself into her hips.

"Maybe. The ways of human men, especially repressed human men, are hard to comprehend," she said, while still trying to keep pace with me.

At this I flipped her. I wanted more. I pulled her to the edge of my bed and bent her over it. I lined up my cock at her cunt and thrust in, showing no mercy in the pace. There was an urgency with Pip that was insatiable.

"Well, luckily for you, you will never mate a human male again. Your cunt is mine," I growled pounding into her at a steady pace. She was so hot and wet for me, I wanted to be touching every part of her. I wrapped my arm around her, snaking my hand up to massage her breast and lightly pinch her nipple. While not much different than breasts of female orkin, Pips creamy skin and dusky pink nipples were exquisite. The little moans she give me as I teased them brought me closer and closer to climax. I circled one with my thumb, then pinched it firmly, just in a way that had earned me cries of pleasure from her in the caverns.

The added sensation was enough to send her over the edge. I felt her muscles locking up, climax impending. She came with a rough sob as I continued to thrust into her. My release followed soon after, I unloaded what felt to be an unending amount of hot cum, feeling slightly dizzy at the power of it. I wrapped myself around her, pulling her into a tight embrace. I wanted her to feel cherished, not just for her body.

"Do you want to—What was it you called it? Spoon? Until my knot softens?" I asked huskily.

"That sounds perfect," she gasped, out of breath.

I lifted her back into bed and wrapped myself around her. We lay together as our choppy breathing evened out.

"What will the day look like?" she asked, stroking my bicep.

"Well, I will have to present our matehood to the elders, which will probably signify some uproar as it is proof that it is possible to have an Elska bond with a human," I explained while petting her hair.

"Do you think they will be upset?" she asked.

"Astrid will not. I wouldn't be surprised if she knows already. As for the others, I am unsure. They know we need more females, but also don't want to displace the females we have," I explained.

It was desperately hard to have this conversation with Pip while still locked inside of her, but I knew there were details she needed. She shifted, pulling my cock with her, causing me to groan unintentionally.

"Agnarr, can you come again while your knot is still hard?" she asked, sounding surprised.

"Já, as many times as you'd like."

"So we can keep going?" she breathed, pushing her ass against my groin.

"We can keep going until you are so full of my cum that it drips down your thighs," I murmured.

Piper pressed her ass back into me, inviting me to thrust again, locked in as I was. I thrust shallowly, unable to pull out completely, while I slipped my hand down her stomach to her curl-covered cunt. I deftly spread her folds and circled her clit as I thrust into her, causing her to grind against me in desperation.

"*More,*" she breathed, pushing her ass against me as I pushed into her.

I picked up the pace, thrusting as much as my knot would allow, with the additional difficulty of lying on my side, all the while stroking her clit. It wasn't long before it hit. She gasped and I felt her muscles clamp down on my cock as she crested her wave of pleasure, panting my name. It was enough to bring me to my own climax, shooting cum into her tight cunt for the second time this morning. I growled and bit down on the flesh of her neck, unable to help myself. If this was how it was going to be with us as Elska mates, maybe Piper was right to worry about how we complete our duties.

As we lay there, both panting and coming down from the crest of our climaxes, a loud insistent bang started at the door.

"Agnarr, you better be alive and well!" Brandr's came muffled through the door.

I chuckled. It was still early, but Brandr would be the first to notice that Sindri was back and tethered to the post outside my room. Piper looked up at me concerned, but I stroked her face, trailing my thumb along her lip.

"It is only Brandr," I said, before giving her a gentle kiss.

My knot had softened to where I could slip out of Piper and I pulled on leggings and ensured Piper was covered before I headed to the door. I opened it to find Brandr, standing with first raised, ready to bang again.

"Good morning, Brandr," I grinned.

"What do you think you are doing? Arriving back and not alerting anyone?" he accused.

"It was late. Everyone was asleep. There was no point in waking everyone to tell them news they'd receive in the morning," I said simply.

Brandr looked over my shoulder to see Piper sprawled in my bed, half asleep.

"And I see you've taken to Piper?" he growled.

"I don't know if it was as much that I'd taken to her, or she'd taken to me," I responded.

At this he grabbed both my shoulders, using my surprise as a weakness, and spun me around.

"Elksa mates," he gasped as he saw the markings running down my spine.

"Yes, it happened on the way to Snaerfírar. When we arrived they confirmed that human women can form the Elska bond. Piper has matching marks." I responded.

His eyes snapped up, noticing my hair no longer in its usually messy top knot, but a plait. He pulled me into a rough embrace, "Congratulations, brother, I know this is what you have long sought for."

"Thank you. She's everything I could have hoped for," I said, looking back to Piper who was curled up in my bed, attempting to look as if she wasn't eavesdropping.

"Piper, do you want to officially meet Brandr?" I called.

"Um, hello," she waved awkwardly, blushing a lovely shade of pink. "I'd love to get up and give you a hug as well, but I'm afraid I'm indecent at the moment."

Brandr barked out a laugh, "You'll soon learn, there's no such thing as indecent here, but I am willing to wait for a proper greeting."

He turned to me, "So, what is next? You know Astrid will want to move quickly."

"I know. I know. But what of the other human women? What happened while Piper and I were away?" I asked quietly.

"They are all awake. We have been keeping them separate from the tribe, awaiting your return, but they growing restless in their rooms."

"Piper will need to speak with them immediately. Can you have Tora and Saela arrange it?"

"Yes, of course. Tora and Saela have been the ones interacting with them the most. And Odin, of course. They are all quite fond of him," Brandr said with a grin.

"Okay, give Piper an hour?" I asked.

"As long as you don't distract her too much. Let's have them meet in the healer's cabin."

CHAPTER 2

AGNARR

I returned to Piper, who lay in bed, hair mussed and face flushed.

"Are you ready to meet all the other human women?" I asked.

"Well, I think getting cleaned up and dressed would probably be a first step. Do you have a bathroom here?"

"You didn't notice it before?" I questioned.

"Uh, nope, didn't spend much time in this room. Too busy panicking."

"Ah, understood. But it is only a sink and toilet, I think we should both have a proper wash before meeting the other women," I said, taking her hand to guide her up.

"Where can we do that?" Piper asked.

"At the sauna," I responded, turning my back to get her something to wear.

"That *what now?*" Piper asked, sounding shocked. I turned

back to see her eyes wide. "You bathe in front of the people—I mean orkin?"

"Um, já?"

"Yeah, nope. I'm not down," she said.

Piper just said two conflicting things. Yes and no? *Wait, what?*

"Pip, you just said yes and no. What do you mean?" I asked

"Sorry, sorry. American slang—well probably Californian slang. Not the point. I am not comfortable bathing with other people or orkin, nor will many of the women. Unless they were on some sort of team sport in high school," Piper explained.

I was perplexed. I'd grown up bathing in our sauna. Orkin were pretty free with their nudity. But if Pip wasn't comfortable with that, I would have to come up with a solution. I looked out the window. It was barely past dawn and unlikely that the sauna would be crowded, but I couldn't guarantee her privacy.

"Okay, so we have two options," I said, looking at her, "One, we can go to the sauna, and hope that there are few orkin there. There are multiple rooms, we can attempt to use one of the smaller ones and hope for privacy. The second option would be to ask to use the pools of one of the older orkin that has a sauna attached to their house."

Piper looked thoughtful but not displeased, "Let's take our chances at the communal sauna," she said.

"You're sure?"

"I can't say that I love it, but if it is going to be part of my life, I guess I can give it a go," she said, giving me a hesitant smile.

"Okay, let's go quickly then before everyone starts to rise." I handed her leggings and a tunic and ushered her out the door.

PIPER

Agnarr and I walked hand-in-hand in the early morning light. Agnarr was the first male that I had bathed or showered or whatever with. I'd never been in a sauna before. I thought they were all just steam rooms. I was hoping for actual water. It wasn't long before we approached a large wooden building with double doors. Agnarr pushed them and they swung open, causing me to gasp. I was faced with what looked like the world's largest swimming pool with steam rising from it. Five older-looking orkin stood in water up to their chests and looked to be deep in conversation. There were several hallways on either side of the pool and Agnarr led me down one. The hallway had three doors.

"There are two steam rooms here and one shower room. They are all used communally, so I can't guarantee no one will walk in, but I think it is unlikely," Agnarr said, opening the door to the shower room.

We stepped inside and I saw a row of shower heads on one wall and a low bench on the other. There were cubbies for what looked like people's belongings and one larger cubby with towels and what looked to be bars of soap. Agnarr began to strip down and I just kind of stared with my jaw hanging open. This was going to be a lot to get used to.

I pulled my tunic and leggings off and folded them, along with my boots neatly into a cubby. I returned to see Agnarr had already turned on two shower heads. He handed me what appeared to be an already-used bar of soap.

"You *share* soap with the entire tribe?" I gasped.

"Já, it's soap. It's self-cleaning. You think we should throw away a bar of soap after one use?" He asked, looking at me like *I* was the idiot.

"Well, no, but—" I stopped. I couldn't even think of how not sharing soap would work. I guess each person could bring soap with them from their own cabin? I looked at the bar of soap, it was clean enough. It wasn't like it had hair on it or anything. Well. I guessed I was doing it.

"Do you have washcloths?" I asked.

"Já," Agnarr nodded toward the towels and I saw there was a smaller pile of neatly folded washcloths. I grabbed one and then stepped under the shower head next to Agnarr. He was already stroking himself down, but I was too nervous about someone walking in to be remotely turned on. I turned my attention to cleaning myself. It did feel good to cleanse my skin of the grime from the road, even though I was on edge. Just as I started to wonder about shampoo I looked to see Agnarr using the bar of soap on his hair. I wondered what they did about conditioner but followed suit. When we were done, Agnarr handed me a towel while he dried himself off.

"Do we put our dirty clothes back on?" I asked.

Agnarr laughed as if that was ridiculous. *How was I to know?*

"No," he said, walking to another cubby I hadn't seen before. He pulled out what looked to be two more towels, but as I unfolded the bundle I realized it was a robe. When I put it on, it was my turn to laugh, it was brown and so long that it pooled at my feet. With the hood up I would look like Obi-wan Kenobi.

Agnarr looked at me, puzzled. "How does everyone bathe on Earth?" he asked, as we gathered our belongings and headed out of the sauna.

Thankfully, we left before anyone else saw us and headed back to Agnarr's cabin while I explained individual showers and bathtubs that were in almost every American home. Agnarr was shocked that everyone had their own shower and bathtub. It seemed that only orkin of high social status had their own sauna here.

When we returned, Agnarr opened the drawers of his dresser one at a time.

"It seems Tora knew what to expect. She has restocked the dresser with fresh clothing for both you and me. My tunics and pants are in here, but there are items for you as well," he said, handing me a fresh set.

After pulling the clothes on, I headed to the small washroom to see if there was anything I could use to do my hair. I felt like a messy bun, as I had been wearing it, probably wouldn't be appropriate for meeting all the new women, but I didn't know how to French braid my own hair. I wasn't stupid enough to ask for a blow dryer and a straightening iron. I opened the drawers and found what looked like the orkin equivalent of bobby pins. A rush of jealousy washed through me at the thought of another woman using Agnarr's bathroom and I fought to tamp it down. We had talked about prior partners. It wasn't until I started collecting some to use that I realized Tora had probably placed them there for me. This was going to take some time to get used to.

I settled for twisting my hair into a crown, an updo that was simple but always seemed to impress people. I looked at myself in the mirror. Still the same Piper. I felt like the last several days had aged me several years but I didn't look worse for wear.

"Pip," Agnarr called to me from his room and I walked out.

"Yes?"

Agnarr's eyes went wide and he rushed me, pulling me into a tight embrace.

"You look so beautiful," he said, "I mean, you looked beautiful before but with your hair pulled back I love that I'll be able to see the lovely pink of your cheeks."

He looked down at me and stroked my face, causing me to blush.

"It's nothing much. I wanted to be presentable for the other women," I explained.

"Well, you look lovely," he said, before kissing my cheek gently, leading me to blush even more.

"Can you..." His voice trailed off and he looked uncertain. "Sorry, I am new to this too. Can you braid my hair?"

"Oh, yes," I replied hastily before heading to the bathroom to get a comb and a strap of leather.

I had Agnarr sit down on the bed. During our bath at the ceremonial pools I had done just a simple braid, but given that he was likely also going to be introduced as the future jarl today, I wanted him to look nice as well. I couldn't French braid *my* hair, but thanks to church camp, I could French braid anyone else's. I finished it up and tied it off with the leather strap.

"Do you want to go see if you like it? I did something a little bit different than the first one. I am going to have to learn more about what kind of braiding your—I mean our—tribe has," I said hesitantly.

Agnarr turned to give me another embrace, "I am sure I will love it, but I will go take a look," he said, before heading to the bathroom.

I followed him, wanting to see his reaction. He looked in the mirror and smiled, his cheeks going a darker shade of green, which I now knew was the orkin equivalent of blushing. When he looked at me I was surprised to see tears in his eyes.

"What's wrong? Do you not like it?" I asked, concerned.

"I love it," he said, embracing me. "I'm just seeing myself for the first time as a mated male. It is a lot to take in."

My heart melted into a puddle. A man who was not only in touch with his emotions but also able to express them. Holy fuck. I stayed hugging him for a minute before pulling back and looking up at him.

"Are you ready to head out? I think it's about time," I asked.

"Já, let's head to Emla's cabin."

CHAPTER 3

PIPER

Agnarr and I walked on the path that curved around the village.

"How are you feeling?" he asked.

"I'm...well, I'm feeling a lot of things right now. I am worried that I am going to be thrust into this position of leadership and the women will already think I have abandoned them. I don't know if they will trust me. On the other hand, I am really excited to see other humans and find out more about them. I think a sense of camaraderie will be good for my sanity."

"Are you ready for this?"

"As ready as I'll ever be. I am used to speaking in front of a classroom so this shouldn't be that different..."

We continued to walk in silence, holding hands. I was oddly at peace as we approached Emla's hut. I had Agnarr, I had the baldrian, and I knew I could manage a classroom. This wouldn't be that different. We approached Emla's cabin and Agnarr paused. He pulled me into an embrace, kissing me gently.

"I am going to stay outside so you can talk, but I am here if you need me at any time, okay?" face etched with concern.

"Yes, that sounds perfect," I said, kissing him again before heading inside.

I let go of his hand and walked up the steps to Emla's hut, taking steady breaths, ready to meet my sisters. I opened the door to find eleven women seated in a circle. Their conversations came to an abrupt halt as I entered.

"Hi," I said shyly, "I'm Piper."

Immediately one of them jumped up and hugged me. She was curvy with a wild mane of curly brown hair. She held me tight before letting go to look at me.

"I'm Billie, we're so glad you are back. Did you get the herbs you needed?" she asked.

I was shocked at her embrace. I was expecting a reserved if not hostile situation, Tora had clearly prepared them well.

"I actually did. So if any of y'all deal with anxiety, we've got meds!" I said enthusiastically.

There were some cheers in the room, letting me know I wasn't alone.

I sat down in an empty chair, completing the circle.

"Okay, so it seems you already know I was left here because of the anxiety meds in my system. The 'bad' aliens decided I was unsuitable for whatever purpose they had abducted me for. Have you all discussed why you were left here?" I asked.

Billie was the first to pipe up. "Yep! We've actually sorted ourselves roughly into categories, in hopes that it would help the tribe."

"Do you feel comfortable going around and sharing?"

There was a unanimous nod. This was going far better

than I had anticipated. Billie, who was seated next to me, started.

"I'm Billie, and I have a hole in my heart. It's minor and doesn't really require any sort of medication, but I guess it was enough for them to deem me unsuitable," she said enthusiastically.

Aside from being alarmed at how readily Billie was accepting her life on an alien planet, I realized I wanted to know more about each woman as we went around. "Can you also add what you did on Earth before you ended up here?"

Billie was quick to respond, "I was the head bartender at a barbeque restaurant. I'm not sure how that will translate into work here, but Tora has assured me that orkin like to drink," she said with a grin.

I could already tell that Billie and I were going to be fast friends. We shifted to the next woman. She was petite and pale but covered in freckles and had a mane of flaming red hair.

"Hi, I'm Ruby," she said with a thick southern accent, "I'm from Georgia and was in my final year of nursing school. We were able to figure out I was left behind because when I was ten I was kicked in the head by one of my father's horses, so part of my skull is a metal plate."

A nursing student will be an enormous benefit to our community, I thought.

"Hi, Ruby, I am glad you are here with us. I think the healer would be very excited to use your experience and skill," I said, smiling.

Ruby smiled back but said nothing, looking down at her hands. We moved onto the next woman.

"I'm Zoey and I'll be honest, it took me a hot minute to figure out why I would be considered undesirable by the other aliens. It was only through Tora's help that we were able to figure it out. I have three metal pins in my ankle. My ex pushed me down the stairs and shattered the bone."

"Zoey, I am so sorry you had to go through that," I say, reaching across the circle, I grabbed her hand.

"I'm getting better every day, but I am definitely not ready to meet any male orkin," she said with a sad smile.

"And that is totally okay," I said, giving her hand a squeeze.

We moved to the next woman.

"Hi, I'm Evelyn," she said in a quiet voice.

"Any thoughts on why you are here, Evelyn?" I asked gently.

"I am on medication for anxiety and depression. I lost both my mother and father prior to being abducted, so I was going through a difficult time," she said.

"I understand, Evelyn. I have severe anxiety and a panic disorder. They have already provided me with herbs that are helping. I am sure we will be able to help you," I said sincerely.

Evelyn nodded, looking hopeful. We shifted to the next woman. She was curvy with a gorgeous smile and pink rosy cheeks.

"Hey all, I'm Virginia, but everyone calls me Ginny. The only reason I can think I have been left is my size. The label the aliens left with me said I was 'not proportional.' I will never fit into a size two or a size twelve for that matter. But if that means I ended up with hot orcs instead of creepy aliens, I am totally down," she said breezily.

I laughed out loud. Ginny was definitely going to be another friend.

"What did you do before you were abducted?" I asked.

"I was in my first year as a licensed therapist and it sounds like we're all going to need some extensive therapy," she said with a grin.

All of the other women laughed, I could tell Ginny was going to be a popular character amongst our abductees. I moved to the next woman. She was tall and blonde, with her arms wrapped around her chest.

"Hi, I'm Lucy. I just finished chemotherapy and radiation. I've had a hysterectomy and I am a cancer survivor," she said simply.

Ooof, that was going to be a lot.

"Are you cancer-free, Lucy?" I asked.

"Yes, as of my last scan, I'm in remission," she said, slightly unfurling from her position.

"Well, I am sure the tribe will do whatever it can to ensure your needs are taken care of," I said sincerely, before shifting to the next woman.

"Hi, I am Joanna, but everyone calls me Joey," she said with a lopsided smile.

She was a short Asian woman with an adorable bob and mini bangs.

"What do you think brings you here, Joey?" I asked.

"Well, it's one of two things. Either my tattoos or my scars. I have tattoos everywhere that can be hidden because I had strict Asian parents. But I also have scars from self-harm in high school. I haven't done it in years, but the scars are still there," she explained.

"Ahh," I said, either could be a valid explanation. "Do you feel like you need any medical assistance?" I asked.

"Nope, I'm good. The scars are from trauma that has long since healed," she said, smiling at me.

"I'm Olivia, but everyone calls me Liv, and I am honestly not one hundred percent why I'm here. I was raised in the foster system. My mom was addicted to drugs and I don't know who my dad is, so I am sure that came up in one of their scans. Maybe PTSD? Anyway, I am a veterinarian and was in my first year of practice and am honestly kind of excited. I am really interested in meeting the hestrs that the orkin use as a means of travel," she said with a hesitant smile.

Olivia was definitely going to be an asset to our team of humans. Between her humble attitude and her experience, she would provide much-needed support. I moved to the next woman in our small circle.

"Hi, I am Diedre. I have fibromyalgia. I am on a cocktail of medications due to my chronic pain," she grimaced.

"Hi, Diedre, we will do whatever we can to ensure that we manage your symptoms," I said, truly believing that the tribe would do whatever it took to ensure she was taken care of.

Diedre nodded quietly, hands folded in her lap. I moved on to the next woman. She was tall, taller than any of the human men I have encountered.

"I'm Gemma, and I'm autistic. I have no idea how they figured that out, but they clearly didn't want an autistic woman, so they dumped me here. But I am pleased. I'll take good orkin over bad aliens any day."

Gemma said this with such acceptance I was surprised. I looked at her, brows raised.

"I'm used to being in uncomfortable situations, this is going to be totally okay," she said lightly.

I smiled, Gemma was going to do just fine. I shifted to the last woman. She looked concerned.

"Hi..." she said, twisting her hands in her lap.

"It's okay," I said. "No one will judge you here, we all come with various difficulties."

She looked up at me hopefully.

"I'm Eleanor, but everyone calls me Ellie. I'm on adderall for ADHD," she said tightly, clearly afraid of reproach, looking up at me.

I laughed, "Girl, before they figured out I had anxiety and panic disorder, they considered ADHD as an option. There's no shame in that!"

Ellie looked slightly more comfortable in her seat, but I knew it was going to take some work for her to open up.

"Do you think they will have medication that helps with ADHD?" she asked hesitantly.

"Well, they had herbs that helped with anxiety, so I'm hopeful for you."

Ellie nodded, looking slightly more comforted. I needed to keep all of these women straight in my head. So we had Billie, Ruby, Zoey, Evie, Ginny, Lucy, Joey, Liv, Diedre, Gemma, and Ellie. I scanned the room, trying to match faces with names, wanting each woman to feel seen and understood. Not only was I the first to wake up, I was to be their jarlin—I never wanted them to think I wasn't considering their needs.

I took a deep breath and looked around the eleven other women, all eyes on me, "So when did everyone wake up?" I asked.

It was Gemma who spoke up first, "Most of us woke up about two days ago?" she said, looking to the other women for confirmation.

All of them nodded in agreement.

"Okay, so what has happened since then?" I asked.

"Well, Tora, Emla, Saela, and Astrid didn't want to introduce us to the rest of the tribe immediately, so they have kept us isolated," Joey responded.

"They told us all about Elska mates and didn't want us to be pushed into anything we weren't ready for," Ruby clarified.

"Astrid said that you'd probably already mated with one of their males and didn't want to push that on us," Liv added.

At this, they all looked at me, clearly waiting for my explanation. I stood slowly, turning my back to them and raising my tunic up over my shoulders. I heard a collective gasp as they saw my mating marks. I stood for a second, before lowering my tunic and sitting back down.

"Yes, it is true. Humans can be Elska mates with orkin," I said. "I didn't go out looking for a mate, but he happened to be in my path on my way to collect the baldrian herbs I needed. He's actually waiting outside right now, should I need anything."

I grinned at the women, thinking of Agnarr waiting for me patiently.

"Have you made any plans with Tora and Astrid in my absence?" I asked.

"We need a permanent place to stay. We know we are displacing some of the male Orkin," Gemma responded. "There was discussion about building the human women a row of rooms to stay in as we become accustomed to Fýrifírar."

"And how do you all feel about that option?" I asked.

"I think it would be best for us not to be living in someone else's home," Ellie said quietly. "I know that it will be quite some time before any of us are ready to take on mates—if ever. I've never considered a permanent relationship."

I gathered the information, thinking on my feet, "Okay, so what would be most important to everyone right now would be a place to stay that doesn't displace anyone else?" I asked.

Eleven heads nodded, so I had an answer. However, I had yet to tell them of what came next for me.

"Has Astrid mentioned that she intends to step down?" I asked hesitantly.

All of the women looked surprised, so that was a definite *no*. Shit. Did I want to explain now or later? I decided to lead with honesty.

"Astrid wants to step down as jarlin. She has chosen

Agnarr as the next in line for her title. This will make Agnarr and I jarl and jarlin of the tribe. I don't know how quickly she intends to move, but I know she's been waiting for Agnarr to take a mate for some time," I explained.

"So you would be the new leader?" Billie squealed, hands over her mouth.

"Well, along with Agnarr, yes. I would be the jarlin and he would be the jarl."

Billie jumped up and hugged me at this, taking me by surprise.

"We will have someone to represent the human women! This is perfect!" Billie exclaimed.

I was surprised to see a lot of heads nodding around the group.

"Would you..." I hesitate. "Would you like to meet Agnarr?"

Eleven heads nodded and I had my answer. I guess it was time to introduce my man to the human women.

CHAPTER 4

PIPER

Agnarr stepped inside, his hulking frame clearly much larger than any of the women present. In the presence of so many human women, he looked so *alien*. He approached me and grasped my hand, immediately steadying my whirling thoughts.

"So. Ladies, this is Agnarr," I said, smiling up at him but feeling my stomach clench with nerves. This was the first male orkin these ladies were meeting.

Agnarr smiled at me, squeezing my hand. I was nervous. I wanted to remember everything the other women had told me. They all stared at Agnarr, some in obvious appreciation of his appearance, some in concern. There was a moment of awkward silence as everyone adjusted to his presence. I shifted uncomfortably.

Finally, Billie broke the ice."How did you know you were Elska mates?" she asked.

"I felt it before we saw the marks, but she didn't believe

me," Agnarr said, giving me a smirk. "I had never felt a draw to someone the way I felt to Piper. I would be with her even if our marks hadn't appeared."

"What if we don't want a mate?" Lucy asked, timidly.

"You don't have to accept the bond," I explained. "If you choose not to accept it, your marks will fade over time, but you will not get another Elska mate."

Lucy looked mildly relieved, as did a lot of the other women.

"So even if we are fated, we don't have to accept the bond?" Zoey asked.

"Yes. You can choose not to accept the bond, but you will not get another Elska mate, based on my understanding," I said, looking to Agnarr.

Agnarr stepped in to provide further explanation.

"Yes. You can reject the Elska bond. It is rare, but it does happen. If you do, your mating marks will fade eventually. The downside is, you will not find another Elska mate, there is only one," Agnarr explained.

"What if we don't find an Elska mate with anyone?" Billie asked.

"You can find a mate of your choosing. It doesn't have to be an Elska mate. Actually, up until Piper's arrival, Elska mates were becoming rarer and rarer," Agnarr said.

"Is there any difference between an Elska mate and a regular mate?" Diedrre asked.

"Well, Elska mates are fated. They do not separate and are more likely to produce young," Agnarr said.

"Is producing young necessary?" Lucy asked hesitantly.

"Definitely not. It is merely one reason orkin cling to their Elska mates. We are low on female offspring so any Elska pairing provides us with hope," Agnarr explained honestly.

Lucy nodded, looking back down at her hands in her lap. She was definitely going to need some help.

"I believe, the next steps for us will be for Astrid to officially step down and for Agnarr and I to take her role," I explained.

"And you sure you're ready for that now?" Diedre asked, looking concerned.

"Well, I was in charge of 150 high school students before this, so it can't be that different, can it?" I attempted for my response to come out breezy, but I could definitely hear the edges of panic in my voice.

Diedre gave me a smile, "I guess you have a point there."

All of the women in the circle looked somewhat comforted. I wasn't really ready to address their concerns one-on-one, but the fact that, as a group, they were willing to accept us as leaders, was a huge deal.

Agnarr asked, "does anyone have questions or concerns?"

"Can you all fill Agnarr in as to what happened while we were gone?" I asked.

I wasn't surprised that it was Billie who piped up first, "Like we said, most of us woke up yesterday, if not the day before."

"And you haven't met the rest of the tribe?"

"No," she said, shaking her head, "Tora wanted us to wait until you returned."

"What have you been doing with your time?"

"Well, we've been comparing the notes left behind by the 'bad aliens' with Tora, attempting to figure out what landed us here," Billie explained.

Eleven heads nodded in agreement. I was relieved they hadn't been exposed to the males of the tribe, not that I didn't trust them, but as soon-to-be jarlin, I was protective of these women. Many of them were definitely *not* ready for a mate, bonded or not.

Given that I had quite a length of time to adjust in comparison to the others, I walked the women through what I had been through since I woke up, leaving out some of the more intimate details. I had just met them, I'd share all the details in time. I ended with bringing back enough Baldrian for several months

"So how are you feeling, now that you have the baldrian?" Ellie asked, fidgeting in her seat.

"Honestly, I can tell it is helping a lot. Hopefully between Emla, Ruby, and Ginny we can find an appropriate way to manage your ADHD," I said earnestly.

Ellie shifted from looking uncomfortable to looking hopeful.

"Ellie, there is no shame in having ADHD. I spent most of my teen years being told to just 'get over' my anxiety. We're here to help," I said.

"Thank you," Ellie said, giving me a watery smile.

"So, what's next?" Billie asked.

I looked to Agnarr, he grinned down at me.

"It seems as if there is a celebration in order. We can welcome the new women and the incoming jarl and jarlin," I said, smiling back at him.

"What do you think?" I asked, looking at the eleven other women, "Are you ready to meet the rest of the tribe?"

They looked at each other. Some of them definitely looked more hesitant than others.

"Will all the males be looking at us as potential mates?" Lucy asked.

I looked to Agnarr.

"I can't lie to you. Many of the males are looking for mates. But with the support of Jarlin Astrid, none of you will be pressured into anything you aren't ready for," he explained evenly.

Lucy took a sigh of relief, as did many of the others. I looked up at Agnarr.

"I think we need to talk with Tora and Astrid about an event where we introduce the women and our matehood," I said.

He looked at me, assessing.

"That is probably for the best. You and I can talk with Tora and Astrid and make a plan for an introduction celebration," he said.

"Are you all willing to meet the rest of the tribe?" I asked.

"As long as there is no expectation of us to jump into bed with the first orc we meet, I'm down," Billie stated.

All of the other women nodded. We would need to warn the males of the tribe not to expect any of the human women to accept an Elska mate bond.

"Okay, we can prepare for that. What other concerns do you have?" I asked.

"I think our primary concern was a longer term living situation, but we've covered that," Gemma said.

"Absolutely," Agnarr responded, "our tribe is in need of females, if a space of your own is something you need in order to feel comfortable, I can't imagine anyone objecting. It will be our priority to make a plan with Astrid and the elders."

"Can they stay in the rooms they are in while we figure out a more suitable location for them?" I asked Agnarr.

"I am sure that won't be a problem. They are the rooms of single males, more than willing to give up their space for single women," he said, grinning.

It was as if the room breathed a collective sigh of relief. I could tell the tension shifted. The women felt they had a safe place to stay and knew their boundaries would be respected.

"So what's next?" Billie asked.

"Do you think you could do an evening meal and an introduction to the tribe?" I asked, ready for either response.

The eleven women looked at each other hesitantly, before silently nodding, one after the other.

"So how about I talk to Astrid and Tora and we figure out introducing you to the tribe at dinner tonight?" I asked.

Eleven women looked at me, nodding, some of them looking more hesitant than others. I looked at Agnarr.

"Can we get some time with Astrid before the evening meal?" I asked.

"Of course, easily," he said, gripping my shoulder.

"Okay, so then it is settled. Tonight, at the evening meal, we will introduce you all to the tribe," I said, trying to keep the nerves out of my voice

AGNARR

Piper and I walked hand-in-hand from Emla's cabin. Her small hand was comforting in mine. She'd done spectacularly with the human women, though I knew it cost her a lot of nervous energy.

"What are you thinking?" I asked, after some time.

"Too many things," she smiled tightly.

"Okay, let's go with what is concerning you the most right now?"

"How pissed is Astrid going to be that I went against her decision and fled to the Snaerfírar Tribe? Is it going to make her think I am not steady enough to take her place?" she asked, voice quavering.

I rolled her question over in my head. Astrid knew *I* had planned to head to the north on my own, but she thought it was to get the herbs for Piper, not to go on a rescue mission.

"I have known Astrid for a long time. She is very fair. I also think she will have empathy considering you were panicking on a foreign planet. Though we haven't had anyone in the tribe with anxiety for some time, I know Astrid has known orkin with who have suffered from it. I'm optimistic that she won't hold your need to run against you. Especially considering how pleased she will be with the outcome."

"Pleased? Why will she be pleased?" Piper asked.

"Astrid has wanted to step down as jarlin for several árs. She wanted me to take her spot, but not until I had taken a mate. She would rather have a pair ruling. And she thought a mate would steady me." I huffed out a laugh.

Piper laughed, "Do you think I will steady you? I don't feel like the steadying kind."

"I think we will make an amazing pair of leaders. I would struggle to manage the changes our tribe is going to have to undergo with the introduction of the humans without you," I confessed.

Piper's cheeks flushed adorably pink, but she didn't voice any agreement. I could tell she was still in her head about everything that had happened.

"Where are we headed?" she asked as we continued to walk.

"To Astrid's cabin."

"Now? Right now?!" She yelped, eyes wide.

"Did you think there would be another more appropriate time?"

"Well, no. But I figured you would have to make an appointment with her or something like that."

I laughed, "For one, that isn't the relationship that Astrid and I have. For two, that isn't how she rules as jarlin. She is there for any tribes member that needs her."

Piper looked thoughtful, "I think that's the type of jarlin I would like to be. I don't think I would like feeling as if there were a barrier between me and those that I lead."

"I feel the same way. I wouldn't feel comfortable acting as if we were above everyone," I responded.

"Well, look at us!" she said, smiling, "we just made our first decision as jarl and jarlin."

"That we did. Deciding *how* you want to rule seems like a good place to start."

We continued down the path to Astrid's cabin. It was near the center of the village, providing all with easy access. The only difference between Astrid's cabin and the other families' cabins was the size of her garden. Astrid loved to grow things and shared all her bounty with the tribe, so no one begrudged her larger plot of land. No one grew a better kúrbít than Astrid. I squeezed Pip's hand as we approached.

"Are you ready?" I asked.

"As ready as I can be," she whispered, leaning into me.

"Welcome back, Agnarr and Piper," Astrid said, one eyebrow raised while still bent over her vegetables, as though she could feel us coming.

"Hello, Jarlin Astrid," I said formally, trying to hide my smile.

Astrid appraised the two of us, garden trowel in hand, "Would you like to join me for the midday meal? I expect there is a lot we have to discuss," she said.

I looked at Piper. She gave me a quick nod.

"That would be very generous of you," I said.

"Alright, come on in. Get yourselves situated in the kitchen while I wash up," she said, already heading for her cabin.

We followed her through her front door and headed to the kitchen, while she headed to her washroom. I had been in Astrid's home enough to know that she had a small table in her kitchen to accommodate guests. There was a more formal dining room attached, but she rarely used it. I absentmindedly stroked the back of Piper's hand with my thumb, loving her soft skin. Her hand looked so delicate in mine. I looked up at her face to see her brow furrowed and mouth turned down.

"Hey, where are you right now?" I asked as I cupped her cheek.

"I am worried Astrid will deem me unsuitable to lead and that you will have to take another mate," she said, her voice tight.

I scoffed, "Impossible. The Elska bond is respected above all."

"Even with a human?" she questioned, giving me a shaky smile.

"Even with a human," I said, leaning in to give her a delicate kiss.

It was, of course, at this moment that Astrid walked in.

"Ah, I see the mating frenzy is still in effect," she said, smiling knowingly.

I pulled away from Piper, feeling the heat rise on my cheeks.

"More or less," I responded, trying to sound neutral about it.

"Is she not pregnant with your young yet?" Astrid asked me pointedly.

Piper responded, "Ah, no. I am on birth control."

Astrid pursed her lips, "Do you not want young?"

"I don't know, honestly. Back on Earth, we don't have Elska mates and I hadn't met anyone that I wanted to spend my life with," Piper responded.

"And now that you know Agnarr is your Elska mate?" Astrid prompted.

Piper's cheeks tinged pink again.

"Well, we haven't had a chance to talk about it yet, but yes, I think I would like to be a mother one day," she said quietly, looking at her lap.

I couldn't let her sit there, uncertain. I grabbed both her hands and pulled her to me.

"I would love to see you grow ripe with our orklings, but only when you are ready," I said, kissing her roughly on the mouth, before returning my attention to Astrid.

Astrid looked pleased that we planned to have young at some point, even if not immediately. She looked sympathetically at Piper.

"I don't mean to imply that you must have orklings in order to be jarlin. However, I know that the elder orkin of our tribe would see your position as jarlin solidified if you were to bear Agnarr's young," Astrid explained.

"I would be honored," Piper said forcefully, looking up from her lap quickly, "I just don't know that I am ready to do it today. My world has been turned completely upside down. I'd like some time to adjust to the idea of being a mother to an orkling. I had reservations about becoming a mother back on my home planet, even if I did meet someone."

Piper spoke with such ferocity I was taken aback. It was easy to only see her anxiety and forget about her claws.

Astrid looked at her, then nodded,"While I can't claim to understand what it would be like to be dumped on another planet and then find my mate almost immediately, your feelings are understandable."

Piper's expression softened a little, "I'm sorry, it is just a lot to ask for me to lead the tribe that might not accept me, a group of women that have been abducted, bear young, and adjust to life on a new planet all at once."

Astrid nodded before turning her attention to the kitchen to make us a midday meal.

PIPER

My stomach unclenched as Astrid looked at me with understanding before turning to prepare us lunch. I hadn't even thought of children with Agnarr and now here it was. I was honest with Astrid. I *did* want children with Agnarr, just not quite yet. I surprised myself with the acknowledgment. Before Agnarr, I had yet to be in a relationship where I wanted to have children with someone. Earth was such a dumpster fire that the idea of bringing children into it seemed almost irresponsible. But with Agnarr, I could absolutely see myself being a parent. Agnarr would be a fantastic father. He accepted my anxiety and my panic attacks and supported me every step of the way. He'd proven himself to be a 'worthy male' in all ways possible. While adding babies into everything we had coming seemed a bit hasty, I had no doubt that I would happily have children with Agnarr at some point.

"Astrid, we were planning on announcing our matehood and our future with the tribe at this evening's meal if you think the timing is appropriate," Agnarr stated.

Astrid continued to move around the kitchen without saying anything. It remained silent for so long I thought perhaps she hadn't heard him. Finally, she approached us with two plates of food.

"Do you plan to introduce the eleven other human women at the same time?" she asked, placing plates in front of us.

"Yes, I think continuing to isolate them would only cause more division," I responded.

Astrid nodded approvingly, "Yes, the tribe is most interested in the human women. The longer we keep them isolated the more of a point of contention it is going to be. Are they ready to meet the entire tribe?"

"I believe so. They seem to have adjusted to the fact that they cannot go home, thanks to Tora and Saela. I think they want to start the process of integrating into the tribe. But you should know, not all human women want to bear young." I explained.

At this, Astrid looked puzzled, "Do you know why?"

"There are quite a few reasons. First, Earth isn't doing so well at the moment. That's putting it lightly. We are experiencing severe climate change which may lead to the downfall of our planet. Many of our governments have become so corrupt that they no longer see to the needs of their people. There are people on Earth who struggle with not having enough food or medical care regularly. The idea of bringing a new person onto a planet that isn't thriving is off-putting for some women. And then, on the other end of the spectrum, some women just don't want to be mothers. They want to pursue their dreams and don't see children in their future. And, now having met them, I know we have at least a few women who have experienced abuse at the hands of their partners. Getting them to trust and produce offspring with anyone will be a challenge," I explained.

Astrid looked taken aback by all of this.

"Would you say Earth is a failing planet?" she asked earnestly.

"I mean, I don't know that I would say it is failing just yet, but it isn't looking great," I responded honestly, images of melting polar ice caps and starving polar bears in my mind.

"Are there any other reasons a human female would hesitate to bear young?" she asked.

"Well, I haven't asked them yet, but I don't know that all human women are interested in males. Some may want to pursue a romantic relationship with a female. Some might not want a romantic relationship at all," I explained.

At this, Astrid looked thoughtful, strumming her fingers against her lips.

"We have orkin that choose same-sex partners, which is not an issue. I can't think of any orkin in the recent past that hasn't wanted *any* romantic relationship, but that shouldn't be a significant problem."

"So, it is only me that must desire to produce young immediately?" I asked, trying to keep the accusation out of my voice.

"As the new jarlin–and a human jarlin at that–showing that a human-orkin child could survive and thrive here, in our tribe, would be important for many of our elders. While I understand that this puts an inordinate amount of pressure on you and Agnarr, it would solidify your leadership," Astrid explained.

I nodded in understanding. I appreciated the frankness of Astrid's explanation of the tribe's dynamic. It didn't seem she cared that much if I had children, but she knew that many of her tribe *would* care. I appreciated her alerting me to this expectation. I looked to Agnarr. I would love to spend a few years just being the two of us, but I knew I wanted children with him. If it needed to be sooner rather than later, I was willing to accept that challenge.

"Astrid, if the tribe is going to expect orklings from Agnarr and me immediately, I am going to need minor surgery. Is that something Emla is capable of?" I asked.

Astrid's eyes went wide, "Why would you need surgery?"

"I have birth control inserted under my skin in my arm. It will need to be removed. If Emla can't do it, I am sure Ruby would be able to. She was in her final year of nursing school," I explained.

"Emla stitches up our warriors—and our wayward orklings—regularly. I am confident that she will be able to remove your birth control." Astrid responded, looking thoughtful.

"Is there something else you are considering?" I asked.

"Well, I would love to give you more time to settle here before you produce young. I know our younger orkin will accept you as a leader, I am just considering what would appease the older generation who are used to our traditions and customs," she explained.

"I would definitely appreciate some more time—especially considering that Agnarr and I have known each other for barely a week. Human couples usually wait a few years before having children," I confessed, looking at Agnarr.

I was worried he would be hurt that I didn't want children immediately; it seemed to be custom to breed as soon as Elska markings were accepted. But Agnarr simply dipped his chin in agreement.

"Piper, I want you to know that I am on your side in this. I understand that you don't want to be bred just for appearances. What I think we can lean into is the fact that not only have your Elska markings appeared, but you have both accepted the bond. The Elska bond is revered in our culture. The elders should respect it," Astrid explained.

At this, Agnarr nodded. Good, he wasn't hurt that I wasn't over the moon about trying for children immediately. I didn't want him to think it had anything to do with how I felt about our budding relationship. And that is precisely what it was—a new relationship.

"So, maybe we could wait a little bit on the removal of my birth control?" I asked, hopefully.

"Let's see how things play out tonight," Astrid said. "I am not stepping down until we have all the tribe unified. Especially knowing that this may be a messy process. But yes, wait on the removal of your birth control for now."

I breathed a sigh of relief. Even though I was ready to

become a mother for the sake of the other women, I was pleased Astrid didn't expect me to start trying to get pregnant immediately.

Astrid shifted the subject, "Have you thought about where you two would like to live?" she asked, looking at Agnarr.

"Mmm, we haven't talked about it. Pip, do you have thoughts?" he asked.

"We won't continue to live in your room?"

Astrid and Agnarr both laughed.

"The tribe is expected to come together to build the new jarl and jarlin a new home. However, we do have some empty cabins if you'd rather see one fixed up. The cabin of the tribal leaders usually offers a bit more comfort than a regular cabin. Like my dining room or garden," Astrid explained, waving her hand toward her garden. "Is there anything specific you'd like in your home?"

My stomach flipped. I had never been asked what I would like in a *home.* I had always just looked for the best apartment in my budget—looking for things like air conditioning and clean carpets. And someplace that took cats. That reminded me, that at some point I would have to ask about pets—a thought for another day. Living in LA, finding affordable housing was challenging. The idea of having no budget for my wants and needs was a little overwhelming.

"Humans aren't used to communal bathing—is there a cabin available with its own sauna?" Agnarr asked.

I looked to Agnarr, eyes brimming with tears. His thoughtfulness was killing me.

"There's Old Harald's cabin? It isn't in the center of the village, but it is easy enough to access. It has its own sauna and is nestled amongst the furutré at the edge of the tribe," Astrid offered.

"I fucking love trees!" I exclaimed, then I clapped my

hand over my mouth, realizing that was a super weird thing to say.

"How many rooms did Harald's cabin have?" Agnarr asked while laughing at my tree comment.

"Four. Plenty of room for orklings," Astrid said, eyes sparkling mischievously.

Agnarr looked at me, assessing, "Would you be comfortable living in a cabin that someone else previously lived in?"

"Mmmm, that is pretty much the standard on Earth, so definitely. I would rather not sleep in a dead orc's bed if that's an option?" I said.

Astrid laughed, "No, Piper, you won't have to sleep in a dead orc's bed."

"Well then, yes! I am good with Harald's cabin as long as you are," I said, looking at Agnarr for approval.

"Piper, you are the one that has been dumped here unceremoniously. Your comfort comes first. I am happy to move into an already established cabin if you would be comfortable in it," Agnarr looked down at me while stroking my neck with his thumb.

"I don't see any reason for the tribe to build a new space for us to live, especially considering the needs of the new women," I said, smiling up at him.

"Well then it is settled," Astrid said definitively. "We will clean out and refurbish Harald's cabin for our new jarl and jarlin."

CHAPTER 5

AGNARR

We left Astrid's cabin, having discussed everything concerning the new human women and our new role as jarl and jarlin.

"What are you thinking?" I asked as we walked back to my room.

"Oh boy, I don't even know—too many things. Um, right now? What should I wear tonight? I am guessing a tunic and leggings isn't what a new jarlin should wear?" she responded, looking concerned.

"I will have Tora come visit. We can figure out an appropriate outfit for this evening—for you and me both," I said, grinning.

Even though I'd had more than a tiår to mentally prepare for becoming jarl, now that it was here, the tiny details would prove to be an unexpected stumbling block. We walked back to my room in silent contemplation. We arrived at my room and I ushered Piper in.

"How long do we have until we have to prepare for this evening?" she asked, intention clear in her voice.

"Not long. It is already late in the day," I responded, taking in the shift of her scent. She was aroused at the sight of my bed, and I would not deny her. I scooped her up and walked her to my bed. I laid her down and leaned over her.

"What do you need?" I asked, my voice hoarse.

"I want everything," she whispered.

I groaned, knowing we were on limited time before Tora arrived to offer us outfit options, but shucked my clothing quickly. Piper removed hers just as rapidly. She was spread out before me in *my* bed like a delicious feast. I could barely hold myself back. But I needed her ready for me. I didn't want to hurt her. I reared over her, leaning in for one of the *kisses* she'd taught me about. I kissed her lips, then down her neck.

"Can I?" I asked hesitantly.

"Yes, I trust you," she responded throatily.

I kissed my way down her body. I stopped to take each of her nipples into my mouth, flicking them with my tongue and suckling them roughly before continuing down her torso, worshiping her body with my lips and tongue. Reaching the juncture of her thighs, I pushed for her to spread wide. She shifted under my ministrations, opening for me. I placed myself at the apex of her thighs, feeling myself grow even harder by the scent of her arousal. My shoulders shoved her thighs open, leaving her little option to object. I knew that *oral*, as she'd called it, was something she was uneasy about. Damn those human men for treating it like a chore.

I looked up at her to see if there was any hesitancy in her eyes, "You're sure?"

"As long as you are," she grinned wickedly.

Instead of responding, I leaned in, licking her slit from

bottom to top with my textured tongue. I felt her shudder under me before she spread her legs even wider, giving me full access to her delectable cunt. I used my fingers to part her lips, before using my tongue to lap steadily against her *clit*, as she had explained it was called during our first encounter. I felt her squirm under me before she tangled her hands in my hair and tugged it to direct me where she wanted. I tried a few different options, before discovering that circling the bud of flesh with the tip of my tongue caused her to pant and writhe. I was desperate to flip her over and sink my cock into her, but I wanted her to come first.

She writhed above me and tried to slam her thighs shut. I knew she was close to her peak.

"I need...I don't know what I need. I'm so close," she gasped.

I continued circling her clit with the tip of my tongue but speared her with two of my thick fingers. She was wet and ready to accept them. Piper gasped at the intrusion but rocked her hips upward. I slowly thrust my fingers in and out of her while continuing to give attention to her clit with my tongue. Her back arched off the bed, as she thrashed her head side to side and I knew I was on the right path. I added another finger into her tight heat, never shifting from the attention I gave her clit.

Without warning, Piper's whole body clenched up, flooding my face with her juices.

"Oh fuck, Agnarr!" she cried out as her orgasm crested.

I lapped at her as she came down before grabbing her by the hips and flipping her. I could wait no longer.

"You are wet and ready. Can you take me?" I asked, barely containing myself.

"Gods, yes, I need you now, Agnarr," she exclaimed, trying to push herself back onto my cock.

I thrust into her welcoming body, groaning at the sensation of her wet cunt gripping me tightly as I slid into her. I breathed through my nose for a moment, allowing her to adjust to my size, including my knot. I stroked her back and massaged her ass as she adjusted to me. I leaned over, covering her with my much larger body, kissing up her neck and nibbling at her delicate earlobes. She gasped, and thrust her ass back onto my cock.

"Harder," she panted.

I pumped my hips in and out, my thrusts growing more foreful the longer we continued. When I was no longer able to hold back, I thrust into Pip fiercely, snarling at the feel of her. Mating with an Elska mate was indescribable. I wanted to bury myself in Pip and inhale her scent forever. Pip panted, pushing herself back to meet each of my thrusts.

"Can I... no, I can't," I started.

"What?" she breathed, "Just ask."

"Can I grab your hair?" I breathed huskily.

"Please!" she exclaimed.

I reached forward, grabbing a fistful of her valhnot locks, and pulled her up against me, my chest against her back, all while continuing to thrust into her. I felt her channel begin to shutter and clamp around me, telling me she was close. I reached around and slid my fingers down her stomach, spreading her lips to find her clit. I circled it with my fingers, as I had with my tongue, causing Pip to shutter and clench beneath me.

"Oh, Agnarr, I'm so close, harder!" Piper gasped.

I left her clit and grabbed her hips with both hands, pounding into her relentlessly, until I felt her clench around me. She let out a ragged sob as she came. I thrust one more time before my cock jerked, unloading spurt after spurt of hot cum into her warm cunt. She collapsed beneath me, completely spent. Locked together with my knot, I laid myself over her, trying not to crush her with my weight, and continued kissing up her neck.

Piper rolled to her side, allowing us to *spoon*, my cock still locked inside her. I wrapped my body around her, appreciating her warmth and the connection between us. I kissed her shoulder blades and neck, unwilling to let her go. I wrapped myself around her, inhaling her scent as I did.

"I'm glad we will have a cabin with its own sauna," she breathed. "With how often I want to fuck you, we will need to bathe regularly."

I huffed out a laugh. "I hope you never lose the desire to fuck," I said, grinning.

After several moments, my knot loosened enough for me to pull out from Pip. I stood and headed to my washroom, and wet a small cloth with warm water, before returning to her. I cleaned her of my cum gently, appreciating the view of her swollen cunt, knowing that I had caused such arousal.

"Do we have time for a nap?" She asked.

"Maybe a quick one. Tonight may be overwhelming, so a nap sounds like an excellent idea," I responded, scooping Piper into my arms. I could already tell that sleeping naked with her was going to be one of my greatest comforts. I held her tightly, feeling her breathing slowly even out. It wasn't long until I followed her into unconsciousness, satisfied and comfortable.

PIPER

I awoke to a knock at the door and it took me a moment to realize where I was. I wasn't in my apartment on Earth, but in Agnarr's room. He was asleep, but holding me closely to his chest, and quietly snoring. I tried not to wake him, while slowly removing myself from his tight embrace. I realized I was completely naked and not fit to answer the door, as the polite, but insistent knocking continued. I grabbed Agarr's tunic and threw it over me. It fell to my mid-thigh, which I decided was enough coverage to answer the knocking.

I opened the door to find myself face-to-face with Tora. I threw myself at her in an eager embrace. I was so pleased to see her. She clasped me tightly to her, returning my embrace before stepping back to look at me.

"I see you have accepted the mate bond with Agnarr?" she asked, smiling.

I whipped myself around and pulled up Agnarr's tunic to show her my Elska marks. Tora gasped, turning me around to hug me again.

"I'm so pleased. How are you feeling?" She asked.

"Nervous, but ready," I said confidently, "I know Agnarr is my mate, and I have no hesitancy about our commitment, but being jarlin is a little overwhelming."

"You will do fine. Astrid won't step down until you are ready, I promise," Tora responded, grasping me into her arms again.

"So, we both need something to wear tonight?" I said, trying to keep my voice low as Agnarr continued to sleep, "Astrid plans on introducing us as the new jarl and jarlin."

"We don't have much time for you to prepare. Let me get you some options and return," Tora said, clasping her hands together.

I looked over my shoulder to see Agnarr still quietly snoring. "I will wake him in plenty of time," I promised Tora.

Tora returned less than an hour later with outfits for us to choose from.

I looked over the outfits Tora provided. I took them to the washroom so as not to wake Agnarr. I examined all the dresses. Everything here seemed to be made of natural fibers or animal hide. The first was way too large. I was swimming in it. The second was a beautiful lavender color but was tight across my hips, causing a wrinkle in the dress. I tried on the last. It was pale blue with long belled sleeves. The neck was a V that showed just enough cleavage to make me feel sexy in a long-sleeved floor-length dress. With the orkin bobby pins, I carefully twisted my hair into another crown, hopefully, fit for a jarlin. I left the washroom to wake Agnarr.

I looked at him, still peacefully sleeping. I didn't want to wake him, but we needed to get ready to present ourselves to the tribe. I sidled up to the edge of Agnarr's bed, still attempting to let him sleep, before climbing in with him. I wrapped my frame around his, breathing in his delicious scent. Agnarr shifted, opening his eyes, to see me draped across him.

Agnarr stirred at my presence, "You're still here?" he asked, clearly still half asleep.

"Of course, I'm your mate now," I responded.

"Has Tora come?" he asked.

"Yes, we have lots to choose from," I explained, not letting go of him.

"How much time do we have?" he asked, huskily.

"Less than an hour," I responded, looking at the outfits Tora laid out for him.

At this, Agnarr immediately sat upright.

"We need to prepare," he exclaimed.

"Hush. I've already done my hair and picked out a dress. I am ready. It is only you that needs to get ready," I explained, soothing him.

"What have you picked for yourself?" he asked, looking my body up and down.

"I'll show you once you are dressed and ready," I responded.

After looking through all the options, Agnarr and I stood in his room, the weight of the evening's events still lingering in the air. Agnarr looked every bit the part of the jarl in a deep green tunic with gold embroidery, and his long hair braided with gold accents. I knew the dress I'd picked out was fit for the occasion, but I was still nervous about how I would be received.

As we prepared to make our way to the bonfire where the tribe had gathered in the longhouse, my anxiety kicked up a notch. The responsibility of being the new jarl and jarlin seemed daunting, and I knew that we had to prove ourselves to both the orkin and human members of the tribe. Given that Astrid had already warned us that I might not be readily accepted, I felt like I was walking into some sort of trial.

Agnarr took my hand in his, giving it a reassuring squeeze. "Are you ready, my mate?" he asked

"I am," I replied, taking a deep breath to steady my nerves. "Let's do this."

We headed towards the longhouse, where Astrid and the rest of the tribe awaited, including the other human women. The evening sky was filled with stars, casting a soft glow on the gathering. We approached the longhouse and entered through the double doors to find all eyes on us, a hush emerging as we walked to the center of the longhouse.

Astrid stepped forward, a smile on her face as she looked at us. "Piper, Agnarr, the time has come to introduce you as our new leaders," she announced, her voice carrying across the crowd.

Agnarr and I stood before the tribe. I could feel the weight of all the eyes upon us. I took a deep breath as Agnarr spoke, "Members of Fýrifírar, tonight marks a new chapter in our history. Piper and I stand before you, prepared to become your new jarl and jarlin."

A murmur of excitement and curiosity rippled through the crowd. The orkin members seemed intrigued, while the human women wore expressions of hope and anticipation.

"We are honored and humbled by your trust and support,"

Agnarr added, his voice steady and confident. "We believe in a future where unity and understanding will prevail, where both orkin and humans can thrive together as one community."

I continued, "Our love knows no bounds, and together, we will lead with compassion and strength, forging a path of unity for our tribe."

As we spoke, I could sense the energy in the crowd shifting. Many orkin looked excited at the prospect of new leaders. Yet, as I looked from face to face, there was a hint of hesitancy in some of their eyes, reminding me that we would have to work hard to earn their complete trust. Agnarr was known and beloved, but I was brand new.

Astrid stepped forward, placing a hand on each of our shoulders. "I have seen the bond between Agnarr and Piper," she said, her voice firm. "Their commitment to each other and our tribe is undeniable. They are Elska mates, proving that humans can mate with our kind. With them at the helm, I do not doubt our tribe will thrive. I will be with them every step of the way as we transition to their leadership."

Her words eased some lingering concern among the elders, and I saw a few of them nod in agreement. It was a small victory, but a significant one. We stepped away from the center of attention to join the feast that had been prepared. Agnarr and I sat with Astrid. As we ate, she fed us tidbits of information, elders who would be on our side, and those who might question our leadership. I tried to take it all in, wishing I had someplace to take notes.

As the celebration continued into the night, with music, dancing, and feasting, Agnarr and I interacted with as many tribe members as possible, listening to their stories and engaging in meaningful conversations. We wanted to show them that we were dedicated to their well-being and valued their input and ideas. I made sure to connect with each of the human women. I wanted to ensure they felt safe and cared for.

As the flames at the center of the longhouse danced, Agnarr and I stood together, looking out at the tribe we were now responsible for. The night air was filled with a sense of hope and unity, and I knew that we were on the right path.

"We have a lot of work ahead of us," Agnarr said softly, his arm around my waist.

"We do," I replied, leaning into his embrace. "But we have each other, we have Astrid, we have the human women. Heck, we have most of the tribe already. I think we can do it."

Agnarr smiled, his eyes shining with love and determination. "I feel like I can do anything with you."

CHAPTER 6

AGNARR

The celebration continued well into the evening with the moon high in the sky. The way Piper leaned into me told me she was exhausted. She had run around making sure every human was cared for and I could tell she was on the cusp of collapse. Without ceremony, I scooped her up into my arms.

Piper squeaked in disapproval, "Agnarr! I can walk!"

"Yes, but you are tired and I am happy to carry you," I replied simply.

Piper looked up at me, ready to protest, but saw the determination in my eyes and seemed to decide against it. Based on what she'd told me, she had never let a male genuinely care for her. This was all new. She melted into me and allowed me to carry her to my room. I hated that I only had a room to provide for her, but that would change soon enough. We entered into the darkness, and I gently deposited Piper onto my bed—our bed—before tending to the fire. My room was chilled without the fire lit, and I wanted Piper to be comfortable. I stoked the fire, adding logs until the room radiated warmth.

I turned to see Piper disrobing from her fancy blue gown and laying it delicately over a chair.

"I know what you're thinking, but we need sleep. Maybe I'll wake you later for some fun?" she said, grinning mischievously.

"Pip," I said sternly, "I don't want you to lose sleep over my pleasure."

"It's not just *your* pleasure," she countered, tugging at my braided mane.

She pulled me into a kiss. She was naked and I couldn't help but think of sex. She continued to kiss me as she climbed me like a tree, legs and arms wrapped around me. I was still fully clothed, but my cock came to attention.

"Maybe we sleep for a while and then meet somewhere in the middle of the night?" Piper suggested.

"That sounds... That sounds good," I stuttered.

I disrobed and joined Piper in bed, spooning. Curling my body around hers, I felt her breath steady as she found sleep. Her even breathing steadied me and I realized how tired I was. It wasn't long before I fell asleep as well.

I awoke to Piper's shoulders between my legs. She kissed up and down each thigh before taking my semi-hard shaft into her mouth. She licked and tongued the head of my cock as I woke up. It was almost more than I could take.

"Wha... What time is it?" I asked.

"Several hours before dawn, we'll have time to go back to sleep," Piper responded, before using her tongue to lick my cock from root to tip.

I shuddered under her ministrations. I didn't think I would ever grow accustomed to her enthusiasm for sucking my cock. But I could tell from her scent that she was aroused. I looked down to see her take my stiff cock into her mouth, swallowing as much as she could take while fisting my knot with her hand. The sight of her mouth around me alone was enough to cause my undoing. I tentatively threaded my fingers through her hair, not wanting to pressure her, but also wanting to set the pace. She moaned at the feeling of my hands in her hair and I took that as permission. I gently led her to a pace and she adjusted, taking as much of my cock as she could into her mouth.

She paused, adjusting, and looked up at me for reassurance before continuing. Though Piper assured me this was normal, I had never had a female pleasure me in such a way, I was completely unsure of myself. I could tell from her scent that she *wanted* to be sucking my cock, but I didn't want her to feel obligated to do so. She slipped her mouth off me, dragging her soft tongue along the underside of it as she did so.

"Do you want me to stop?" she asked.

"No, gods, no. I just don't want you to feel as if this is something I expect of you. I lick you to get you wet and ready for my cock. You do not need to do that," I responded.

"Agnarr, do you enjoy..." she paused, looking for the right words, "Do you enjoy licking me? Or is it just to get me ready?" She asked.

"Yes, gods yes," I responded without hesitation. "You taste absolutely divine and watching you shatter under my tongue is everything to me," I babbled. I was probably not making any sense.

Piper nodded and then looked at me with one eyebrow raised. "Well?"

"Well, what?"

"Well, can't you see how it would be the same for me? To taste you and see you come, just because I enjoy giving you pleasure?"

Well, that made it sound entirely logical, but maybe I wasn't able to be logical about this.

"I guess I am not used to a partner wanting to do something solely focused on my pleasure," I said, pausing, "which you aren't used to either?" I reached out, running my fingers through her hair.

Pip looked off for a minute before nodding, as if reliving old memories, then sighing. "Yes, it is hard for me to have you focused on me." She paused and looked up at me, "But you are making it easier every day just by being you."

I shifted and pulled her up from where she was between my legs, to bring her into an embrace, "Luckily, we have a lifetime to learn each other's wants and needs."

Piper wrapped her small body around mine, nuzzling my neck, and sighed.

"What are you thinking?"

"Do you think we will be able to convince the tribe to accept me even if we wait a bit before having children? I want to spend some time with just you," she asked hesitantly.

"If that is what you want, I will fight for our ability to wait. I can't say I would mind a few seasons with you all to myself before we prepare for orklings," I said, smiling down at her.

She continued to hold me tightly, "Not only would I love nothing more than a few seasons of just you and me, but I also don't want to be accepted as jarlin just for the young I might bear. I want to be accepted on the merits of my ability to lead. I am willing to be viewed that way if it will help the other human women, but it feels like a slap in the face," she explained.

"What?!" I reared up over her in anger, "Who slapped—"

"No, no, no," she cut me off, pressing her hands to my chest. She stroked my chest and down my arms, trying to soothe me, before speaking, "'Slap in the face' is an American saying. It means insulting. No one slapped me, but they definitely insulted me. I have years of classroom and leadership experience. If I can manage seventeen-year-olds, break up fights, and teach them something every day, I think I could lead a tribe of humans and orkin. Accepting me only for my womb is pretty fucking insulting."

I was taken aback. I hadn't thought about it like that at all. I looked at Piper with eyes wide. It was almost as if she could see me unraveling how that would feel.

"Pip. I'm so sorry. I want you as my mate, whether or not we can have young," I say earnestly.

"I know. I believe you. But I am going to need your support with Astrid and the tribe to adjust expectations. These human women are not just here to have children," she said softly. "Some of them may never be ready to have children."

I looked at Piper. Really looked at her. I understood her concerns. I knew I would do anything to ensure she and the other human women were treated fairly. This would be my greatest challenge as the new jarl.

"I will do whatever it takes to ensure your women are treated as whole individuals—not just vessels for orkin young."

Piper captured my mouth and kissed me deeply as she slid her body over mine, making her intentions clear. The conversation was over. I had acknowledged and addressed Piper's very logical fears and now she required physical comfort.

"What do you want, Pip? Do you want something slow and languid or hard and fast?" I asked.

"I want you to make love to me," she said wistfully.

I rolled us so I was on top of her. Aware of our size difference, I supported myself on my elbows so as not to crush her.

Pip wrapped her legs around me, inviting me into her

warm cunt. I pushed upward, sliding my cock between her folds, both of us letting out a low moan as I seated myself completely. I looked into her eyes, checking for any hesitancy. She pulled me in for a kiss, slipping her tongue between my lips. At the same time, she dug her heels into my ass, urging me to thrust.

"You don't need to be so worried, I know I am smaller than you but I promise, feeling every ridge and texture of you and the pressure of your knot feels absolutely incredible," she said, still breathing the same air from our kiss.

I kissed Pip again, before slowly pulling all the way out and then thrusting back in. Piper dug her nails into my shoulders and I steadily thrust in and out of her welcoming body, worshiping the gasps and moans that she made each time I pushed into her warm heat. I remained steady, not wanting to rush our pleasure, as I slowly pumped into her. I felt her channel begin to flutter around me as I continued to surge into her, slowly ratcheting up my pace. I watched as Piper threw her head back, sighing in pleasure as I slid in and out of her. I tried to keep a steady pace, but the gasps of pleasure coming from her made it incredibly difficult.

I grabbed her face without changing my pace, "I want to see your eyes as I make you come."

Pip's large green eyes met mine, and she nodded. She wrapped herself around me more tightly, embracing the treatment I gave her. It was difficult to stop myself from slamming into her with all of the force I possessed, but a small part of me was still afraid I would harm her. She tightened my cock as I continued to plunge into her. We were both close. I changed my pace, driving into her more forcefully as she dug her nails into my shoulders. She looked me in the eye, uttering only one word.

"More."

"I don't want to hurt you," I groaned.

"Agnarr, I won't let you hurt me. Stop holding back."

I was already so close to the edge that it didn't take much for me to unleash myself completely. I let go and pistoned myself into her slick heat. I continued to plunge into her. My sack tightened, ready for release, but I wanted her to finish first.

"Oh god, Agnarr," she gasped as I continued to thrust into her.

I didn't know the god she was exclaiming to, but I wanted her to think only of me. I slid my hand down her stomach. I continued to thrust into her while slipping my fingers between her folds and pressing my calloused thumbs against her clit. I circled the bundle of nerves with my fingers while I continued to thrust. I tried to maintain eye contact, but it seemed to be more than she could bear.

Piper wrapped herself tighter around my body, biting into my shoulder. I felt her cunt flutter as she came and came and came. I continued to pump into her, knowing she was already spent. As Piper's body trembled and convulsed in the throes of her climax, I held her close, kissing her tenderly as I felt her pleasure ripple through her. Her nails dug into my shoulders, and she buried her face into my neck, her breath coming in ragged gasps.

I slowed my pace as her orgasm subsided, giving her a moment to catch her breath. Our bodies remained connected, and I held her tightly, savoring the sensation of her soft skin against mine.

"Are you alright?" I whispered

Piper lifted her head, her green eyes sparkling with post-orgasmic bliss. She smiled up at me, a mixture of contentment and desire in her gaze.

"I'm more than alright, Agnarr," she murmured, her voice a soft, husky whisper. "That was... incredible."

I leaned down to capture her lips in a tender kiss. As our

kiss deepened, I continued to move within her at a slow, steady rhythm.

I pulled back slightly, breaking our kiss but keeping our gazes locked. "Tell me what you want, Piper," I said, my voice rough with desire.

She looked at me with a mix of desire and vulnerability, her fingers threading through my hair. "I want to feel you come inside me, Agnarr," she whispered, her cheeks flushed.

With a growl, I increased my pace again, my hips moving in a rhythm that drove both of me closer to the edge. Piper's moans filled the air, and I held onto her as I felt my control slipping.

As the intensity of our lovemaking heightened, I focused on the sight of Piper beneath me, her flushed skin, her lips parted in pleasure. With a final thrust, I felt my release surge through me, my body shuddering as I spilled myself inside her. Piper's name tumbled from my lips as I buried my face in the crook of her neck, overcome by the waves of pleasure coursing through me.

We remained locked in each other's embrace, our breaths slowly returning to normal. Eventually, I shifted to lie beside her, pulling her close so that we were tangled together beneath the blankets.

Piper nestled against me, her head resting on my chest. We lay there in the afterglow, our bodies intertwined, hearts beating in synchrony.

"I love you, Agnarr," Piper murmured.

"I love you too, Piper," I replied, pressing a soft kiss to the top of her head. "And I will cherish every moment we share together."

As the first light of dawn began to filter through the window, we drifted off into a peaceful slumber, wrapped in each other's arms.

CHAPTER 7

AGNARR

"No," I stated, arms crossed over my chest.

The elders looked at me surprised.

"No, the human women will not be treated solely as a means to bear young. Some of them don't even want orkin," I explained. "A few simply cannot bear young. They will not be treated as wombs for as long as I am jarl," I said firmly.

The entire council sat at the long table at the head of the longhouse, having a meeting after the prior night's proclamation. Astrid still remained at the head of the table, while I was seated at her right side. Some of the council members nodded their assent at my statement regarding the human women, others looked shocked. Some of the older males looked downright angry.

"And what of your mate?" Magna, the elder from the smithy asked.

"She is willing to bear young at her own pace," I said, frowning severely.

"And what does that mean?"

"It means she'd like some time with her mate before she welcomes an orkin child," I said fiercely.

"And what does *that* mean?" Alvis, the elder in charge of the hestrs jeered.

"It means she'd like some time to fuck me just for fun before I put an orkling in her belly," I said fiercely, shooting daggers at the elders questioning me.

"So you're that good at sex?" he mocked.

"Já, *I am*. Apologies that you aren't," I said, attempting to hold back my sneer.

Astrid said nothing, allowing me to run the meeting, but she quietly placed a hand on my knee. I shook my head, attempting to regain my composure. I was set to be jarl. I needed to represent the entire tribe, not just those that agreed with me.

"The human women are willing and ready to accept our way of life. This alone should be celebrated as we are low in females. Further, I would expect us all to want Fýrifírar's name to be known as the tribe that was willing to accept refugees with open arms. However, the women will not join us readily if we are only after their ability to produce more orkin. I think all of us can realize this importance," I said sternly, looking at all of the gathered orkin.

Piper hadn't joined me at this first council meeting. It was probably for the best, considering she would have reached over the table and throttled some of the elders. We sat at an impasse, the older orkin wanting nothing to do with the human women if they wouldn't immediately bear young, and me, along with Astrid and some of the other elders, refusing to budge.

It was Emla, the elder who represented the healers who finally broke the silence, "I know that you and Piper are Elska mates, I've seen the marks. We know that with orkin, this means that young will be produced. Do we know if there is any difference with humans? What if she is unable to carry an orkling?"

I looked at Emla thoughtfully, she was one of the elders that I already had on my side. She would also be the elder to deliver any of these young. I understood her concerns.

"Piper and I saw proof of a human orkin pairing while at the Snaerfírar tribe. There is a half-orc named Steve. His mother arrived here many ars ago, just like the Piper and the others were, dropped unceremoniously and left behind," I explained.

"And what did this *Steve* look like?" Magna asked.

"What does it matter what he looked like?"

"Well, we don't want half-breeds running around looking like these weak, pale females."

There were no words for my anger at Magna for the disrespect he was spewing toward these women. And for what reason? He was far beyond his prime. His own Elska mate had given him several young and passed peacefully a few seasons ago—then it hit me. He had three sons, all of mating age. He wanted grandchildren that looked like orcs.

"You can't be serious," I said deadly quietly.

I was ready to lunge over the table, but Astrid got there first. She stood quietly, and while petite, she radiated power. A hush fell over the room at the command she held, "Jarl Agnarr and Jarlin Piper are set to step into power in three cycles of the moon. I advise that you fall in step with their plans for the future of Fýrifírar or risk being expelled from the tribe," she said quietly. She had one of those voices that could command attention even at a whisper.

It took all that I had to keep my jaw from dropping to the table we were seated around. Astrid had just declared that unless the tribe supported Piper and me, they would be expelled. I never expected such support. As Astrid turned her back on the elders leaving the longhouse, all eyes were on me.

"I can't say I will be sorry to see any of you go, but for what it is worth, Steve looks like an orc. He has slightly smaller tusks, rounded ears, and a leaner build. But he is all orc, right down to the green. Many of the human females are willing to take mates. Some of them will likely form Elska bonds. But they will not be treated as if that is their only value," I said before I stood and left the longhouse myself.

I took a walk, telling myself not to do anything foolish like I had the last time I felt this overwhelmed. I'd felled a tree on Piper... though that scenario hadn't turned out particularly badly for either of us. I flushed remembering her pink lips around my cock.

This was going to be harder than I thought. Even with Astrid's unwavering support, introducing the human women threatened to tear the tribe in two. I leaned against the external wall of the longhouse, breathing deeply. I felt the pressure of the line we had just drawn—*I* had just drawn. We might lose some elders with our expectations of integrating the humans. But from what I knew and understood of Piper, I couldn't let these women be treated as nothing more than vessels for young. She'd explained to me that some of them wouldn't even be able to carry young—willing or not.

I'd have to tell Piper the full truth of the contents of the meeting and I knew her rage would be unbridled. While her anxiety made things difficult for her at times, she was a force to be reckoned with. I laughed to myself at the thought of her banging down Magna's door before punching him square in the face. I headed to Astrid's cabin. We needed a plan.

PIPER

The women and I came to some sort of unspoken agreement that the healer's cabin was where we felt most comfortable. Instead of sitting in the weird group therapy style we'd sat in last time, we all kind of gathered where we felt at ease, most of us with a mug of tea in our hands. Apparently, Fýrifírar had no coffee, which was definitely going to be a problem. I was already feeling withdrawals from my venti iced sugar-free vanilla latte with 2% milk. In some ways, I *was* a basic white girl. No shame.

I cleared my throat, in an attempt to call the meeting to order. All eyes immediately settled on me.

"Okay, I don't want to go full-on teacher-mode with y'all, but we need to have a chat," I said seriously.

There was a mix of concern and enthusiasm throughout the group.

"I've met with Jarlin Astrid, and Agnarr is currently meeting with the elders. The Fýrifírar is willing to welcome us in with open arms, but there are going to be some hang-ups that I know are going to be an issue," I explained. "Over the last few decades, their population has become predominantly male. They don't know why, but they are in desperate need of females. While the younger orkin are willing to accept all of us, no strings attached, some of the older orkin are insistent that the human females take orkin mates immediately."

The tension surrounding that statement was palpable. Gemma and Zoey looked as if they might pass out.

"Agnarr and I have had long talks about this because, as the leader, they expect me to bear orklings immediately. And the thing is, I am just not down. Not even a little bit. I want children. I want children with Agnarr. But right now? Hell no."

There were many sighs of relief as I continued to explain.

"It seems as if most of the orkin roughly our age and younger have no issue with us integrating into the Fýrifírar tribe, it is the elders that take issue," I said.

"Ahh, so the boomer-orkin aren't fans of us?" Ginny said.

The room erupted in laughter.

"Pretty much," I said laughing, "the boomer-orcs aren't fans."

"I think we can take them," Joey said confidently, leading to more laughter in the room.

"I know that it is a hard burden to bear. Neither I, nor Agnarr, nor Astrid, expect you to take a mate or get knocked up anytime soon. But it is the battle we are up against," I explained.

"I mean, I wouldn't mind getting knocked up," Billie said openly. "I've wanted babies since I was young. I am happy to be the example of what a human and an orkin can produce, given I find the right mate."

I laughed. Billie, sitting here, next to me, willing to bear the orkin babies of someone she'd yet to meet. I wanted to wrap myself around Billie and sob into her shoulder. And I wasn't even a hugger.

"Agnarr is with Astrid right now, meeting with the elders. I know he is defending our rights and asserting that we are unwilling to be more than wombs for orkin babies. What else is on the table?"

"Well, given that we aren't going to be forced to be knocked up right away, we should continue focus on getting us a permanent place to stay," Lucy said quietly.

"Okay. I am going to let Agnarr fight the battles on bearing children. I am going to fight the battles of giving you all a home," I said.

Heads nodded around the room.

"I want you to know, I feel like between you and Agnarr,

we are well taken care of. We know you are trying your best to see to our needs," Diedre said.

"Thank you, it means a lot. Even though I have experience in leading a classroom, this is brand new. I am incredibly grateful for your faith in me and your faith in Agnarr. I know there are a lot of hurdles to overcome, but Agnarr and I will support you every step of the way," I said to the room, trying to catch each woman's eye.

The air in the room seemed to lighten with the proclamation.

"So, it will be okay if we aren't ready for mates or children?" Lucy asked.

"That is what Agnarr, Astrid, and I are fighting for. Acceptance without expectation." I said bluntly.

All of the women looked at me, hopeful they'd be treated as more than just brooding mares. I felt the enormous weight on my shoulders and was ready to stumble home into Agnarr's arms. It was late and all of the conversations had been heavy. My anxiety had me exhausted. I wrapped up the meeting, leaving the women to their own devices. I wasn't sure where to head. Our new home was under construction, with all of our belongings still in Agnarr's old room. I hesitated as I considered where Agnarr would hope to find me. I decided to head to our new home.

CHAPTER 8

PIPER

*T*he rooms of the old cabin were stripped bare to give Agnarr and I the option to put in what we wanted. I couldn't help but marvel at the home nestled among the trees—laughing to myself at saying *I fucking love trees* in front of Astrid. Well, if I had to pick an alien planet to land on, one filled with trees was definitely a plus. But as I looked around I saw the barren space I realized above all else, we'd need a bed. We'd also need chairs and a dining table and other pieces of furniture to fill the space. There wasn't even a place for me to hang my cloak.

I stood in the entryway for a moment, wondering what to do with myself. Someone had left the lamps lit at the end of the work day as if they knew we would be by to look at our new home. I wandered from room to room silently planning things out in my head. I was no interior decorator, but having such a large blank canvas was amazing. I immediately picked out what would be our bedroom. It was the largest room, with a balcony that faced the forest and its own toilet.

None of the rooms had their own showers, but the back of the house had a sauna on the ground level. I thought about a bed that would fit both of us easily and wondered if asking for a four-poster would be too much. I'd always wanted one as a teenager and with the amount of wood that Fýrifírar had, it didn't seem like much of an ask. There was an odd small room off the main bedroom that I couldn't figure out for a moment—then it hit me—it was for a baby. Oh, this baby business was going to be on everyone's minds for a long time. I decided not to look too deeply into it and left the main bedroom.

I inspected the three other bedrooms, all smaller but still spacious. Orcs were larger than humans, so it made sense. So with the tiny nursery and the three bedrooms, there was room for at least four children. *Did I want four children?* I thought, absently stroking my soft, but relatively flat stomach. Four seemed a bit much. Maybe we could use one of the rooms as a playroom.

I returned downstairs to find an office off of the living room, which would be excellent for Agnarr's duties. I pictured him sitting at a large wooden desk, going over paperwork. Then, without warning, the image of me bent over the desk popped up. Well. That was definitely something I was interested in. As if summoned by my thoughts, he opened the front door and walked in.

He took one look at me and made his intentions clear. We hadn't seen each other all day and the mating frenzy was still in full effect. My thoughts of being bent over a desk—hell, bent over anything, were abundantly obvious with the look I returned. I took a step up the stairs toward what would be our bedroom, but Agnarr was faster than me. He grabbed me around the waist, nuzzling himself into my neck.

"I've missed you," he said huskily.

"It's been less than a day, how did you know I'd be here?" I panted, knowing I'd missed him just as much.

"It was still too long. I'm still learning you, but I thought you might be anxious about our new home" he murmured as he scraped his tusks down my neck to the edge of my tunic, leaving goosebumps in their wake.

He slipped one hand under my tunic, squeezing my breast and teasing at my nipple with his rough fingers as I gasped. I wanted him. He yanked my tunic, splitting it as if it were spun from spider webs and pulling it off me. He spun me, and I stood two steps above him, my breasts at his eye level. He kneaded them with his warm hands and then pinched each nipple, causing a shudder to slip down my spine. He took my nipple into his mouth and sucked it as if he expected to draw milk from me. I gasped and grabbed each of his pointed ears, pulling him closer as he plundered my chest.

"More," I keened.

Agnarr flipped me again. I was still in my boots and leggings. He massaged the globes of my ass before grabbing the back of my leggings and forcefully ripping them from me. I gasped.

"Agnarr, you can't ruin all of my clothing!"

"Why not? I will soon be jarl, I can have new clothes made for you every day if I want," he said with a chuckle.

"Well still, it's a waste!" I exclaimed but was immediately distracted by his lips and tusks on my neck. He pulled me down the steps until we lined up, given our height difference. I felt his bulge push against my backside and sucked in a breath.

"There's no bed here, Agnarr," I said, as he trailed kisses down my shoulder.

"Does there need to be? I don't recall there being a bed when I fucked you in the caves."

I listened in anticipation to the sound of him shoving his pants down behind me. Before I knew it, he was dragging his hard and already dripping length up and down my slit readying me for him. I felt my juices slide down my thighs, at the feeling of his leaking cock, knowing what I was in store for. He slowly pushed into me, as I grabbed the stair railing with one hand to steady myself. Agnarr grabbed one of my legs by the underside of my knee to spread me wider as he slid home. I gasped at the fullness of his knot breaching my entrance. He held me there for a minute, allowing me to adjust to his size, while still breathing against my neck.

"Are you ready?" he breathed.

"Absolutely."

He slowly pushed further into me, stretching me wonderfully as I held onto the stair railing.

"Oh, Agnarr. Oh, fuck," I gasped.

He pulled back out completely before plunging into me again. We were here, in our new unfurnished house, fucking on the staircase. This knowledge ratcheted up every feeling I had. *Our* home. Together. Agnarr grasped me around the waist, his thighs, brushing against mine as he pumped into me harder and harder. I could feel myself coiling tighter and tighter around him as he pummeled into me. Every stroke of his magnificently ridged cock hit all the right places. I was almost embarrassed to come so quickly. But Agnarr's cock and the ferocity with which he pumped into me had me close to the edge.

Keeping a hand on the banister to steady myself, I moaned in pleasure as he hit all the sensitive spots inside me, cherishing the attention he gave to my body. He leaned in to lick the sweat from my neck. I inhaled his scent, musk with a hint of the furutré trees that surrounded the cabin. I wanted to turn completely to kiss him, but his broad hands digging into my hips prevented me from doing so.

"Agnarr, I want to see you come," I gasped, as he ratcheted up the pace.

I knew he was close, but he didn't complain as he slid out of me completely. He flipped me with ease, seating me on the stairs, while he kneeled before me. The soft glow from the candle-filled chandelier made his skin appear an even darker shade of green. I admired his bunching muscles and his beautiful skin. He pulled me in and devoured me, licking and sucking on my lips. I lifted my legs, wrapping them around his waist and pulling him to me. With him one step below me, he was at a perfect angle to slide in. I gasped at the length of him—again. I would never grow tired of the shock I felt every time he plunged into me. He kneaded my breasts and plucked at my nipples causing me to gasp.

"These were all I thought about today, even during our council meeting. My thoughts strayed to your perfect tits and your pink cunt," he breathed, thrusting in and out of me relentlessly.

"Mmm.. And I thought of your ridges and your knot as I met with the human women. I hope some of them are willing to take mates—if you are any indication of what they are in store for, they will not be disappointed," I responded.

Agnarr fell forward, placing his hands on the stairs on either side of my head, rutting into me. I could no longer hold back my gasps and moans. I keened underneath him and was suddenly very grateful that our new home was a fair distance from any neighbors. As Agnarr grunted and groaned into my neck, I was well aware of how much noise we were making. His pace quickened and I wrapped myself more tightly around him, digging my heels into his muscled ass.

"Oh, Pip. Oh fuck," I felt the kick of his cock as he spurted into me, right as I uncoiled beneath him. I felt my crest pulse from my center out to my limbs, almost choking me with the bliss of coming around him. Agnarr pumped into me, once, twice more, before he was completely spent. I felt his cum fill me, dripping out onto the stairs of the home we hadn't even moved into yet.

"This mating frenzy isn't going to stop until I'm pregnant, is it?" I asked breathlessly.

"Um, based on what I know—no, no it will not."

"Well, I hope you're up for a couple of years of good fucking."

"I have no complaints."

Agnarr nuzzled into my neck, breathing deeply. I must have smelled as good to him as he did to me.

After a few moments of letting my breathing come down, I asked, "So what now? Are we going to sleep on these stairs? There's no furniture in this cabin."

Agnarr chuckled into my neck before kissing along my jaw, "I shall carry you back to our shared room, the floor is not fit for the new jarlin," he whispered.

True to his word, he lifted me, covering me with my cloak, and carried me all the way across the village to our room. I used the washroom to relieve myself and clean up the copious amounts of cum I was still getting used to. I returned to the bedroom, to find Agnarr thoughtfully pulling down the bedding for me. He looked at the cloak I wore to travel from our new house to his room and said, "You won't be needing that. I already told you I will have no clothes between me and my mate in bed."

"I know, I know. You've said. And as long as you continue to keep me warm and be up for midnight romps, I have no complaints. I can't help myself if I roll over in the middle of the night and find your semi pressing against me."

"I feel like that's a fair deal," he grinned wickedly at me, before heading to the restroom to clean himself up.

I took the opportunity to climb into the large bed, luxuriating in the softness. I was no camper. The trip to the Snaerfírarr tribe was not my favorite. I wanted a bed and running water. I wanted a shower. I was glad to see that I wouldn't have to go without these in my new home. After a moment, Agnarr came back and turned down the gas lamps, before joining me in bed. He snuggled into me, spooning me as I had taught him.

He reached up to stroke my hair.

"Tomorrow is going to be another busy day, isn't it?" I asked.

"It is. We have over half the elders with us, but I would prefer if we were a united front. I will be meeting with them and Astrid again," he explained.

"Is this something I should be present for?" I asked.

"No, Astrid and I are representing the needs of the human women well. I have no doubt in her support. What would you like to do tomorrow?" he murmured, kissing across my temple.

"I'd like to get our home ready. I would like to spend the day on my own meeting with merchants and carpenters, decorating our new home. Do you... have the money to spend on that?" I asked hesitantly, unsure of how finances worked on this new planet

"Well, the jarl and jarlin are paid a stipend which should cover the cost of everything you could possibly want. But if you need access to funds right now, I have been saving all of the wages I earned as a guard for when I finally met my mate. Tell any shopkeeper to put it on my tab and they will know I am good for the payment, regardless of the cost," he said, still peppering me with kisses. "Is there anything specific you would like?"

"A four-poster bed, if it's not too much trouble? I've always wanted one."

"That doesn't seem like much of an ask," he said simply,

"though I should let you know, Osif is the elder of the carpenters and he is on the fence about the human women. You may need to use some of your impressive charm on him."

"Does he have anything against us?"

"No, but he is not of mating age and doesn't want to see disruption to the tribe, I think he will be easy to win over."

"Ahh," I said knowingly, "I can handle that. And you'll be meeting with the entire council again?"

Agnarr sighed, "Yes. As it stands, of the nine council members we have, five of them are willing to accept the human women with no expectations. We have two on the fence and two that are firmly against. We don't *need* a unanimous vote, but both Astrid and I would like one," he explained.

"Who is against?" I asked, curiously.

"Magna, the elder of the smithy, and Alvis the elder that cares for the hestrs," I said.

"Are there any specific reasons?" I asked.

"Magna has three sons of mating age. He doesn't want his grandchildren to be 'human,'" Agnarr said with distaste.

"Well, then his sons can be the few that get no fucking mates. Gross. We have prejudiced people like that back on Earth. I am used to it, but it doesn't make it less repulsive. You met Steve! He looked almost fully orkin!" I said, outraged.

"I have a feeling Magna and his sons may leave, and to that I say, fine. We have other apprentice smiths that can step into his role. It's his choice. He will have to step down if he is unwilling to accept the humans," Agnarr explained simply.

"And what of Alvis?" I asked, "Can I cozy up to him?"

"He doesn't have any stake in the situation, he never had young, too focused on rearing hestrs. He doesn't want to get involved in anything that is going to cause turmoil. I think he would be easy to convince, but it should be me that approaches him," Agnarr explained.

"Okay, so tomorrow I need to charm Osif while you meet with the the other elders?" I asked.

"I fully believe in your ability to charm him," Agnarr responded, his voice growing sleepy.

I tucked myself further into his embrace, realizing we could continue our conversation in the morning. I let my eyes flutter closed and gave in to the exhaustion that my anxiety had been pressing into me all day. I was grounded by Agnarr's steady breathing and it wasn't long before sleep took me under.

* * *

I AWOKE TO THE SUNLIGHT, desperately needing to pee. The morning air raised goosebumps on my naked skin. I tiptoed across the bedroom, the floorboards creaking under my steps.

In the small washroom, I sighed in relief. I used the toilet and rinsed my hands and face in the sink, taking a moment to study myself in the mirror. My hair was a mess, but I had a contented glow about me.

Returning to the bedroom, I paused to admire Agnarr's sleeping form. The sun streamed across his muscular green back as he lay on his stomach, arms clutching the blankets. I felt a surge of love for this gentle orc who had changed my life.

Unable to resist, I bent down to plant a soft kiss on his shoulder. He murmured happily but didn't stir. I nestled back under the blankets, pressing close to steal his warmth. In the morning we would start building our new life together as jarl and jarlin, but for now, I treasured this quiet intimacy. I matched my breathing to his, letting his rhythmic snores lull me back to sleep.

I awoke again to a shift. I felt Agnarr begin to stir beside me as the morning light filled his room. He rolled over, blinking the sleep from his eyes before focusing on me with a smile.

"Good morning," he rumbled, his voice still thick with sleep.

"Good morning," I replied softly, reaching out to caress his cheek.

He caught my hand and pressed a kiss to my palm, then shifted closer to wrap me in his strong arms. I settled against the solid warmth of his chest, cherishing the sense of safety and belonging I felt with him.

We lay together silently for several minutes, simply enjoying each other. Agnarr traced lazy patterns on my back while I listened to the steady beat of his heart. No words were needed in this peaceful moment.

Eventually, Agnarr cupped my chin, tilting my face up to meet his lips in a tender kiss. I melted into it, savoring the connection between us. When we finally broke apart, Agnarr's amber eyes were full of love.

"I can't imagine a better way to start the day than waking up with you," he murmured.

"Neither can I," I agreed, snuggling impossibly closer.

There was much work to be done today—meeting with carpenters, starting plans for the leadership transition, and adjusting to our new home. But all of that could wait a little longer. Right now, wrapped securely in Agnarr's embrace, was exactly where I wanted to be.

Agnarr rolled me on top of him, pulling me close and peppering kisses down my neck. He massaged my ass as I sat atop him, admiring the view of my breasts.

"Do we have time for this?" I asked, breathing in his scent.

"I will always make time for this," he responded, pulling me to him.

I felt Agnarr harden beneath me, his cock pressing into my ass cheeks.

"If we are going to continue at this rate, I may need to start doing some stretching exercises," I said, with a laugh. "I'm not used to fucking every day."

Agnarr looked astonished.

"Everyday. Twice a day. More than twice a day is normal for orkin," he said.

"Oh boy, I am definitely glad we picked a place with its own sauna," I responded.

Agnarr looked at me confused.

"If I don't keep all my bits well cared for and clean it can lead to infection," I explained.

"Ahh, I don't know if female orkin have the same necessity, but I wouldn't be surprised," he responded. "The sauna is a very popular place for our females."

"There's only so much cum a girl can take before she needs a thorough cleaning," I said, laughing over him.

"Well, you will have your own sauna and you can bathe as many times a day as you see fit," he said, before pulling me to him and rubbing his nose against mine. I planted my hands on either side of Agnarr's head and leaned in to plunder his mouth. I licked his lips as he parted for me, allowing our tongues to tangle together. I moaned as he teased my lips and tongue with his, already feeling myself ratcheting up. I was wet and ready for him, and the sun wasn't even fully in the sky.

CHAPTER 9

AGNARR

I lay in my bed with Piper astride me, my cock urgently pressing against her ass. We'd already had fucked on our new staircase, but I intended to fuck her in every room of our new home, sauna included, whether or not there was furniture available. I gripped her soft hips with my hands, engulfing her waist. For now, my small bedroom would have to do.

"Is this what you want?" I asked. It was still well before the morning meal. The idea that Pip was awake and ready for another round was foreign to me. I knew orcs had a lot of sex but Pip was human—and this was more need than I had ever experienced. I didn't know if it was Pip or the Elska bond, but we both seemed insatiable. She was already on top and I felt the slickness of her cunt against me, ready for my cock.

"Are you sure we have time? Before your meetings?" she

asked breathlessly—a question that was on her lips every time we came together.

"I arranged to have all of our meals delivered for the time being—we have plenty of time," I assured her.

She moaned at this, rubbing her slickness up and down the length of my cock.

"Can you fuck me hard before breakfast arrives?" she breathed, hands on either side of my head.

"I think I can manage that," I responded, sliding my cock up and down her slit.

I grabbed my length and pushed it into her welcoming heat, causing her to gasp at the intrusion. Knowing we were short on time, I thrust up into Pip, groaning at the tightness of her. She kept her hands on either side of my head, kissing me deeply, showing that she wanted all that I had to offer. I pulled out almost all the way before thrusting again. I'd never felt such perfection. Piper's tight warmth accommodated me in a way that was simply breathtaking. We moved in unison, Piper meeting every one of my thrusts with one of her own. The thought of a lifetime to learn each other's needs and wants was almost overwhelming.

Piper and I had barely a vika together and had already established an open and honest line of communication. The idea of a life with her was almost more than I could bear.

"Pip, you feel incredible, I want you always. Just you," I breathed as I pumped into her. I wanted to fill her with my cum and put an orkling in her belly, even though I knew we agreed to wait. My orkin instincts demanded I fuck her until I put a baby in her womb.

Pip met each of my thrusts with enthusiasm, giving as much as she got. I reached between us, using my thumb to flick against her sensitive center, causing her to cry out.

"Oh, Agnarr, oh fuck! Don't stop," she cried, as I continued to pound into her.

I continued to thrust into her with her head resting against my shoulder, barely able to contain the mounting pressure.

"Pip, I am going to come inside you," I said breathlessly,

"Absolutely, Agnarr, I want your cum. No one else deserves it," she responded, unwavering in her pace.

I ratcheted up my rhythm at her approval, pistoning into her mercilessly, living for her cries and moans. Her legs tightened around my waist, inviting me to delve even deeper. I felt her lock up around me, her muscles going taut.

"Yes, that's it," I whispered as I continued to hammer into her.

Pip let out a final cry before coming around me and collapsing against my chest. I thrust, once, twice, and three more times before emptying myself into her welcoming body. She wrapped her arms around me, holding me tightly.

"I really don't know how we are going to get anything done with how often I want to fuck you," I murmured, stroking her hair.

"We will have to learn to be quick," she said, grinning. "Twice a day, however we can fit it in, deal?"

"Deal," I said.

Piper slipped off as my knot loosened, heading to the washroom to clean up. We'd made an absolute mess and breakfast was due to arrive any minute. I heard the running of the tap and the flush of the toilet before Pip reemerged.

"I need to throw something on before breakfast arrives," she said, pulling at the drawers of the dresser we currently shared.

Pip pulled another hand-me-down tunic. I would have to speak to the town tailor. The new jarlin needed clothing befitting of her title. I headed to the restroom to clean myself up, letting Pip settle herself in front of the fire. I heard a knock on the door while I was in the washroom. I headed back to the main room and found Pip situating a breakfast tray on the small table in front of the fireplace. She had a bowl of hot gautr in her hands and was grinning at me.

This was my life. It was everything I had hoped for and I could barely comprehend it. I wanted to fall to my knees in joy, seeing her there, in nothing but a tunic, eating breakfast in my room.

"So shall we review the schedule for the day again?" I teased.

"You're meeting with Astrid, then with the council," Pip responded seriously. "I'm meeting with the carpenters to discuss the needs of the human women and furniture for our new home. Are you sure you don't want me at the council meeting?"

"I will eventually, I just want to set the stage before I bring you in. Things are still strained. They know you are managing the human women," I explained.

"I am happy to do whatever you think is best for the tribe," Pip responded over her tea, "I trust you."

We continued to eat our breakfast in comfortable silence.

"Do you think we can do this?" Pip asked.

"I know we can," I responded without hesitation.

PIPER

I took a deep breath as I entered the carpentry workshop, feeling all eyes turn to me. As Agnarr's human Elska mate, I knew I was viewed with suspicion by the orkin. But I held my head high, determined to earn their respect.

"Good morning," I greeted them warmly. "You must be Osif?"

"Já." The elder orkin eyed me warily.

"I've come to discuss lodging needs for my fellow human women who have joined the tribe. They feel as though they are displacing other orkin, having to live in the homes of unmated males. I, along with Jarlin Astrid and Jarl Agnarr, ask that you build proper dedicated housing for the humans. Astrid has agreed that we will cover all costs associated with building the homes."

The carpenter's face remained stoic. "You're asking quite a lot. The Fýrifírar tribe has never accepted outsiders before."

I nodded understandingly. "I know it will be a lot of work to house these women, but I think they will bring valuable contributions to the tribe. It is at the direction of Jarlin Astrid that I am here."

The carpenter hesitated, his expression doubtful. After a long moment, he finally replied. "It will be as Jarlin Astrid wishes."

"Thank you," I said sincerely. "I know the women will be grateful for any consideration. If we could move onto the housing for Jarl Agnarr and I?" I asked, plastering on my best teacher smile.

The carpenter grunted in a way that I took as an invitation to go on. I was going to win this orc over if it was the death of me. I had an idea.

"Can you keep a secret?" I whispered.

The older orc looked up at me suspiciously.

"It depends on what kind of secret," he said, squinting at me.

"I want a surprise for Jarl Agnarr," I said conspiratorially.

"Já, and what would that be?"

"You know the tree he felled on me?" I asked.

"Já, that rumor has gone around the tribe quite a few times now. Jarl Agnarr is not trained in felling trees, as I am," he said, puffing out his chest.

"That is abundantly clear, otherwise I wouldn't have ended up under it," I laughed, boldly placing my hand on his.

He almost smiled at this. Almost.

"Well, I would like to use that tree to build some of the furniture in our new home, namely our bed, our dining table, and our mantlepiece," I leaned in closer to whisper, "I think Jarl Agnarr views that tree as a mistake, but I view it as the beginning of our relationship. I want to surprise him with it."

Osif looked at me for a long moment before sighing, "Já, that is an excellent idea. Agnarr would be pleased with the use of that tree. There is enough wood to use it for all that you ask."

Thrilled, I reached over Osif's bench and hugged him. He went stiff and looked startled but didn't pull away. Even though I still wasn't big on hugging, but I felt like I was playing the role I needed to play with him. Eventually, I separated from him, a smile plastered on my face. I went on to describe a four-poster bed and other furniture needs for the home. I detailed everything down to the desk I intended to be fucked over repeatedly. Osif nodded at all of my requests, noting them down on his ledger.

"You know, my grandfather was a carpenter?" I asked.

Osif looked up at me, curiously, "Was he?"

"Yes, he designed my bookshelves when I was a child. I loved to read. I never had enough space for my books."

"We can build you bookshelves for your new home with Jarl Agnarr, as many as you'd like," Osif murmured.

After a bit more conversation about the needs for our new home I left. I'd done it. Osif was mine. I felt lighter. I had Osif on my side. My mixture of enthusiasm and vulnerability apparently worked just as well on orkin as it worked on American teenagers. I cackled inwardly at how easy it was going to be to win over these gruff older orkin.

AGNARR

I sat back and listened as the elders bickered amongst themselves. We had five elders firmly on our side. Jodis, the elder from the teachers, was young. She wanted more students and had no reason to disrespect the human women. Emla had already met Piper and several of the humans, she was 100% in support of integrating the human women into our society. Inga, Astrid's daughter, was in training to be a healer, so it was no surprise that the healers would side with Astrid's wishes. Emla's voice, as the elder representing the healers, would not be dismissed. The elder representing the cooks, Runa, had no reason to disagree with Astrid and was a close friend. She was easy to convince. Astrid's son Ottar, worked in the kitchens. The head of the guards, Vott, wanted more women for his warriors to mate with—regardless of race. He was pro, no questions asked. Bram, the head of the businesses in town, saw new families as new businesses. He had no objections.

This left us with Osif, the head carpenter, Magna, the smith, Vigot the elder representing the farmers, and Alvis, the manager of the hestrs. They varied in their level of support. Osif was absent from the meeting, having more pressing duties to attend to–namely meeting with Piper. The carpenters and Vigot were on the fence, whereas Alvis and Magna were firmly against including human women in the tribe. Magna didn't want his sons breeding with human females. Alvis was just a grumpy old orc, set in his ways. It would take a lot to charm him into accepting the human women. Astrid stood, leading to a hush falling across the room.

"Okay, as we stand, we have five elders in favor of fully accepting the human women. We have two on the fence, and two firmly against? Is this correct?" She asked crisply.

"I believe that is correct," Magna stated, crossing his arms over his chest, making his displeasure clear.

"Well, I would prefer a united front, but I will take a majority," I said genially. I couldn't help but step into the conversation, "We will have unanimity, don't you worry. Many of you have not met Piper or the other human women. If after you meet them, you haven't changed your mind, you are welcome to leave. Or keep your hands to yourselves."

CHAPTER 10

AGNARR

I entered my room to find Piper sipping tea at the low table in front of the fireplace. She looked up to me, grinning, eyes ablaze.

"What's for lunch?" I asked, looking at the tray spread before me.

"It appears to be meat pies and fresh fruit. I was waiting for you before I dug in," she said, still holding her tea.

I sat and assembled plates for the both of us. I put two meat pies and a mountain of fresh fruit on Piper's plate before handing it to her. She laughed.

"Eventually, you'll learn what a human is capable of eating," she said, handing me one of the meat pies, before taking a bite of the other.

Piper could eat, as she had clearly shown me, just not as much as an orc. She demolished the meat pie, humming in satisfaction, before turning to the fresh fruit. She finished about half of it, before leaning back in her chair, clearly filled to the brim.

"You will want for nothing," I promised.

"Trust me, you'll know if I am hungry. I promise," she replied.

"So what did you get up to today?" I asked.

"Not much. Just convinced Osif to join us in integrating the human females into the tribe," she said, beaming at me.

My eyebrows raised, "And how did you do that?" I asked.

"That's for me to know and you to find out," she said mischievously, "All you need to know is, you don't need to worry about Osif."

I leaned back from my plate. That was another elder in our favor, due to the work of Piper. We had the teachers, the healers, the cooks, the businesses, the warriors, and now the carpenters. That left the smiths, the farmers, and the keepers of the hestrs. It was six to three. The farmers and the keepers of the hestrs wouldn't be a problem. It was Magna, the head of the smithy, I was worried about. I wondered if I could go around him. He had three sons on the hunt for a mate, perhaps they wouldn't share the same views as their father. If they wanted a mate, they would have to be willing to accept our terms. I rolled it over in my head and decided it was a fight for another day. I had the midday meal to spend with Piper and didn't intend to waste it.

I watched as Piper carefully finished her fruit, "what are your plans for the afternoon?" I asked.

"Well, I was going to meet with the human women and tell them about the strides I had made with the carpenters," she said happily.

"Do you have time..." I hesitated, this was all new to me even though we'd talked about it, "do you have some time for me?"

She looked up at me grinning, "I always have time for you. What did you have in mind?"

"Um... Anything? Everything?" I said hesitantly.

"Ooh, I could be up for everything. When is your next meeting?" she asked, grinning.

"I am meeting with Astrid in two hours," I said.

"Ooooh, that is plenty of time for everything. Strip," she demanded.

"Wh-what?" I stuttered.

"Strip. All your clothing, off. Now," she said imperiously as she moved to remove her own clothes.

I shucked my leggings and tunic faster than I thought possible. I found myself naked in front of Piper, my hard cock jutting out from my body.

"We have two hours?" she confirmed, also completely naked.

"Já," I breathed, looking at her pebbled nibbles and her cunt covered in valnot locks.

"We can accomplish plenty in two hours," she said, before giving me a clear command, "in the chair."

"Wh-where?" I stuttered.

"In the chair," she said matter-of-factly, pointing to the chair next to the fireplace.

Unsure of her intentions, I walked to the chair by the fireplace, utterly nude, my cock leaking at its tip. I sat, looking at Pip, unsure of what to expect. She approached me in the chair, before settling in front of me on her knees. She grasped my cock with her small hand, pumping me up and down, causing me to groan in pleasure.

"What do you want, Agnarr?" she said, hand still around my cock.

"I want your mouth," I said hesitantly, almost afraid.

"Then my mouth is what you will get," she said, breathing over my cockhead.

She then licked me, from root to tip, pausing to lave at my knot, before taking me into her mouth. I shuddered, it was almost more than I could bear. I gripped the arms of the chair, trying to steady myself. Breathing through my nose, I steadied myself as I watched her suck and lick my cock with urgency. I could smell her arousal ripening as she sucked me. Even though what Pip referred to as *blow jobs* was becoming a regular part of our routine, it still felt like an out-of-body experience for me. I was unused to being on the reciprocating side. It was heady and unsteadying. I could tell from Piper's moans and her smell that she was aroused by licking my cock and it put me in dangerous territory. I was going to come before I was ready if I didn't stop her. I fisted her hair, pulling her off of me.

"I want to cum inside you," I said, heatedly. Even with her birth control, I wasn't wasting an ounce of my cum in her mouth.

"How do you want me?" She asked

"On your knees," I responded without hesitation.

She turned on her knees, exposing her backside to me, looking back at me in expectation. I curled over her, nudging her to spread wider to accommodate me, feeling her breathing kick up a notch. I looked at her, spread wide for me, and could barely contain myself at the view of her perfect cunt and ass, begging to be plundered by me. I grasped my leaking cock and smeared it up and down her slit, relishing as she panted beneath me. I slowly pushed into her, grasping her soft hips with both hands. Piper gasped at the intrusion but pushed her ass back toward me. She was eager for my cock and I was willing to give it.

I had never been with a female long enough to learn their wants and needs. Piper wanted me untamed and honest with her in bed—or, anywhere for that matter. I was trying my best to show her what I wanted and what I liked, all the while not expecting too much. The fact that Piper had let me pull her hair was almost more than I could handle. A female willing to consider *my* desires? It was almost beyond comprehension.

"What do you want, Agnarr?" she breathed, as I thrust into her.

"I want to cum inside of you, again and again," I responded, thrusting at a punishing pace.

"Then do it. I want your cum, all of it," she breathed, spread wide for me.

I breathed through my nostrils, inhaling her scent, barely capable of the permission she gave me. My hands gripped her hips even more fervently, as I thrust into her. I felt my ridged cock drag along her inner walls and it took all of my restraint to keep from cumming immediately. I thrust again, living for her moans and keens of pleasure.

I continued to piston into Piper, my hips slamming against hers. She moaned and whimpered, her hands gripping the armrests of the chair as I filled her with each powerful thrust. Her wetness and warmth enveloped me, driving me wild with desire.

Piper's gasps and cries filled the room, and I couldn't get enough of the sound. It was unlike anything I had ever experienced, this raw and intimate connection between us. I leaned over her, pressing my chest against her back. My mouth found her neck, and I kissed and nibbled at her skin, savoring the taste of her sweat.

She responded eagerly, arching her back to meet my thrusts, her nails digging into the armrests of the chair I had been seated in. The sensation of her body clenching around me pushed me closer to the edge.

"I'm close," I groaned, my voice filled with desperation and need.

Piper's breathless reply came in whisper, "Cum inside me, Agnarr. Fill me with your cum."

With those words ringing in my ears, I gave into the overwhelming pleasure building inside me. My hips moved faster, my thrusts grew more erratic, and finally, I couldn't hold back any longer. I buried myself deep inside Piper, my cock pulsating as I released my hot, thick seed into her, filling her completely.

Piper cried out as she felt my climax, her own body shuddering with pleasure beneath me. We clung to each other, panting and trembling, riding the waves of our shared ecstasy.

As our breathing slowed our bodies began to relax and my knot loosened, I pulled out of her gently and kissed her tenderly on the shoulder. She turned to face me, a contented smile on her lips, and I couldn't help but return it.

"Thank you," I whispered, my heart filled with gratitude for the newfound bond between us.

Piper caressed my cheek, her eyes filled with affection, "anytime" she teased.

CHAPTER 11

AGNARR

*W*ell, midday fucking was definitely something I would happily get used to. I sat, admiring Piper in nothing but a tunic, as we enjoyed the rest of our meal. I was grateful that I'd had the foresight to have all of our meals delivered for the time being—knowing that meal times might be the only time we got alone.

"So what's on the schedule for the afternoon?" Pip asked, looking up at me.

"I'd like to sit down with you and Astrid," I said.

"Are you worried?" She asked.

"No, but I want us all on the same page," I explained.

"Well, that seems like an excellent plan," Piper said, before she leaned in and kissed me. "Does Astrid have time for us?" She asked.

"Astrid wants to step down. She will make whatever time is necessary in order to ensure a smooth transition,"

"Well then, I guess I should put on some pants," Pip said, standing up.

Once we were dressed, we headed to Astrid's cabin.

We found Astrid, as she always was–in her garden. She looked up at us, smiling.

"Let's have some tea," she said, before heading into the house.

We followed her into her kitchen, settling once again at the small table. She hustled about her kitchen, preparing food and drink. She then placed a cup of tea in front of Piper.

"It will prevent pregnancy. I know you're on human birth control, but you reek of sex. Better safe than sorry," she said, as she continued to bustle about her kitchen.

Piper turned bright pink but took a large sip of the tea. I watched as she fidgeted, knowing she was intimidated by Astrid. I slid my hand onto her thigh under the table, squeezing her leg, just to let her know I was there.

While Astrid moved around the kitchen, we caught each other up on the status of the elders and Pip alluded again to the fact that she had won over Osif.

Astrid looked surprised but didn't question Pip further. She laid out an afternoon spread of cookies and pastries while continuing to rummage around her kitchen. Finally, she sat with Piper and I. She looked at Piper, "So what's the deal with the human women?" she asked bluntly. I was pleased that she was comfortable enough to drop the leader facade.

"Well there are a couple of camps they fall into," Piper explained, unaffected by Astrid's direct question. "We have the first group. They are ready and willing to take a mate and are happy to be here. Then we have the second group, they want a mate but are hesitant about bonding immediately. They will definitely need some time to adjust. Then we have the final group. This group is going to be the trickiest. These women have been abused by human men and are hesitant to take on any partner," Pip explained.

"Abused how?" Astrid asked.

"Well, for most of them it's primarily emotional, but there are some physical–"

"You mean their partners physically harmed them?" Astrid asked, cutting Pip off with a shocked expression.

"It is more common than we'd like to admit, but yes, physically abused by their partners," Pip explained.

Astrid looked as if she were going to be sick.

"How so?" she asked, gripping the arms of the chair she was sitting in.

"Well, we have one woman who was pushed down the stairs by her partner, leading her to break her ankle in several places. We have a few women who were forced into sex by their partners. We have some states where that isn't against the law," Pip explained.

Astrid blanched at this explanation, "So there are places on Earth where women are expected to submit to their partners, regardless of their wants?"

"Uhhh... Yeah... And unfortunately, a lot of them still exist in what we would call 'civilized' society. I know we have at least one female ex-military who was taken against her will by her fellow soldiers. " Pip said.

"Well… That is not how we operate here," Astrid said, clearly at a loss for words.

"Astrid. In the United States, which is where all the women are from, we've never even had a female leader. It has been almost 250 years and every leader has been male. Male and elderly. Consideration given to the human females is something they are going to be overjoyed about but hesitant to put their faith in," Pip explained.

I could tell she was welling up and trying to hide it. My grip on her thigh tightened under the table.

"We were all raised in a society where the voice of a man was stronger, more powerful, and more trusted than that of a woman," Pip said.

"So you've never had a female leader?" Astrid asked.

"Never. Actually, they are in the midst of stripping away women's rights even more right now," Pip explained. "Our government is full of crotchety old men who are trying to limit the bodily autonomy of their female constituents."

Astrid looked both confused and disgusted. For a moment she didn't say anything. She opened her mouth, then closed it, as if reconsidering.

"I have been jarlin of Fýrifírar for several ars now. We don't know why our population has shifted toward male dominance, but our females have always had their rights respected. I am sorry, but its seems as though your homeworld lacks an understanding of what its females need. I don't want to insult your home, but you will be treated much better here," she stated.

"It is going to take a lot of convincing for some of the humans that they will be respected as equals. For some of them, their trauma is the reason they were left here by the bad aliens," Pip explained.

Astrid nodded over her cup of tea, looking thoughtful.

"But you have many that are willing to take on mates?" she asked.

"Several. I have one that wants a baby right now. I think the others will be less intimidated as they see their peers form Elska bonds."

"Well, that is better than I expected. I have been presenting the human women as off-limits until they show interest. The fact that there are some that are already interested will bode well for our council meetings," Astrid responded.

"Do you think it is time for me to join the meetings?" Piper asked.

"I think it would be good for you to be at today's afternoon meeting. Osif will be there," Astrid said.

Pip nodded, eyes wide, "I'm ready," she said.

"Are you ready to take on Magna?" I asked, knowing he'd pose a problem.

"Don't you worry about Magna, love. I may have anxiety, but I also have claws," she said, stroking my thigh under the table.

"Well, then it is settled. One hour from now. You will both be at the council meeting?" Astrid asked.

"Yes, we'll be there. We are going to oversee the renovations of our new home, we'll return for the meeting," I said.

PIPER

This was it. My first council meeting. I knew they'd been prepped to expect me, but I was still nervous. Agnarr, Astrid, and I went over who would be in attendance, in detail. I was as prepared as I could be. As I entered the longhouse, I was pleased to see several familiar faces. I had already met Emla, Osif, and Astrid. Osif even gave me a small smile as I sat down. I scanned around the room, trying to see if I could match faces with names that Agnarr had given me.

I recognized Jodis immediately, she was the youngest. Agnarr had informed me she was the elder who represented the teachers and was firmly on the side of the humans. She had a warm smile and gave off kindergarten-teacher vibes. I looked to her left to see the only other female, who had to be Runa, the elder of the cooks. She was older than Astrid, looking almost frail. I knew from what Agnarr had explained that Astrid's son was set to take over the kitchens when Runa stepped down. It appeared as if that would be sometime soon.

I only recognized Osif out of the rest of the elder male orcs. I looked at Astrid as she seated herself at the head of the table with Agnarr to her right, and me next to Agnarr.

"I think some introductions are called for," she said crisply.

The orc to her left smiled genially as she turned to look at him. He looked to be in his sixties, with graying but tidily braided hair.

"I'm Bram, the elder representing the businesses and merchants of Fýrifírar. Welcome Jarl Agnarr and Jarlin Piper, I am excited about your plans for the future of our tribe," he said with a warm smile.

I nodded, returning the smile. Agnarr had explained that Bram was already on the side of the human women. I was genuinely happy to meet him. We moved to the orc next to him. It was Osif.

"I believe Jarl Agnarr and Jarlin Piper already know me," he said gruffly, "but I am the elder of the carpenters."

"Lovely to see you again, Osif," I said genuinely.

Next to him looked to be one of the most displeased orkin at the table. Without missing a beat I said, "You must be Magna?"

The orc's eyebrows raised, "And how would you know that?" he asked.

"You look as if you'd rather be anywhere but here and clearly feeling a bit on edge that so many of the others are willing to accept newcomers ," I said.

"Ah, so the human females are mind readers?" he said, curling up one lip.

"Nope, just used to the patriarchy," I said coolly.

"The what?" he asked coldly.

"The patriarchy. Back in the States, many of the men in

our society, and sadly some of the women, hold patriarchal values—the idea that men should be in power and women should be largely excluded from decision-making. So tell me, Magna, is it a human problem that you have, or is it a female problem?" I asked bluntly.

Magnar spluttered over his response to my very direct question, "I—I don't have a female problem. I have served under Jarlin Astrid since Jarl Ulf passed on," he exclaimed.

"Yes, but you've never given me the same deference you gave Ulf," Astrid said in her own icy tone.

Ooh, this shit was about to go off.

"Have I ever questioned your decisions?" Magna asked Astrid.

"No, but you've made it clear that you've served under me begrudgingly since day one," Astrid said.

Magna looked as if she'd slapped him.

"Wait. Hold, please. Jarlin Astrid lost her mate young–tragically–and then you *questioned her leadership?* What a fucking tool," I spat under my breath.

At this Magna looked genuinely perplexed.

Agnarr leaned over and whispered, "Pip, I think you may have used too much American slang in that one, no one has any idea what you just said."

I covered my mouth with my hand to stifle my laughter. Even in a serious moment like this, confusing the orkin with American jargon was still my favorite thing. I took a breath to compose myself, before looking directly at Magna.

"So, Astrid lost her partner and since then you've disrespected her repeatedly. Further, you believe females should not be in leadership, regardless of race?" I asked Magna crisply.

Magna shifted in his seat, looking uncomfortable, unable to meet my gaze.

"Ahh, I am used to males like you. I met plenty of them

during my career. Know this. As long as you continue to hold these misogynistic views, your sons will find no mates, orkin or human. Astrid has assured me that this tribe is founded on equality between males and females. Jarl Agnarr and I won't have you tarnishing its reputation," I said.

Now Magna looked as if *I'd* slapped him.

"Misogynistic?" he asked, clearly perplexed.

"Yes, misogyny. Contempt for women. Clearly, you have it in spades. Next," I said moving to the orc to the left of Magna.

Magna spluttered, trying to compose himself and I raised my voice over his stuttering, "I said, *next*," ignoring Magna completely.

AGNARR

It was all I could do to keep my jaw from dropping to the table. Piper had just eviscerated Magna and then stepped over him as if he were nothing. I knew she was a force to be reckoned with, but seeing her command a room like this was something else entirely.

Vott, who sat next to Magna, smiled at Piper easily, "I'm Vott. I represent the guard. We are happy to accept the human women in any capacity they choose to join us."

Piper eyed him skeptically.

"My warriors want mates, but they know that they will have to adhere to the expectations of the new jarl and jarlin to even be considered as appropriate mates for any of the humans," he explained.

Piper nodded in approval, "I appreciate your perspective, Vott. Your warriors will do well with the humans if they adhere to your guidelines."

Pip moved on to the next elder, Vigot. Vigot was the elder

representing the farmers. I knew he was on the fence, but he looked pale after the treatment Magna received.

"I—I'm Vigot," he stumbled over his words.

"And what group do you represent?" Pip asked.

"I represent the farmers," he said, gaining his footing and sounding more confident.

"And how do the farmers feel about the addition of the human females to the tribe?" Pip asked.

"Well, we are concerned about having more mouths to feed during the winter months, but have no other concerns," Vigot answered

"And if we had human females that could aid in your farming?" Pip asked.

"Then we would have no concerns whatsoever," Vigot responded. "Extra help would make it easier to feed extra mouths."

Pip nodded, giving Vigot a small smile, "Then we will have no issues. I know there are at least a few of the humans who would love to lend a hand to farming at Fýrifírar.

I watched as Pip's eyes moved to the next orc, Alvis. Alvis was going to be a challenge.

"Hello, I'm Piper. We have yet to meet. Who do you represent from Fýrifírar?" she said cordially.

"I represent the stable orkin, we breed and care for the hestrs," Alvis explained.

"Ah. Well, I have met one of your hestrs first hand. Sindri and Agnarr saved my life. I want you to continue to do your good work. Do you have anything against incorporating the human women?" Pip asked.

"Honestly, I am torn," Alvis responded, "I don't like to see disruption in the tribe, but I am interested to see what the human women have to offer."

"So the fact that we have a veterinarian—or an animal

healer—amongst the human women, would appeal to you?" Pip asked pointedly.

Alvis looked surprised, "You have healers devoted to animals on Earth?"

"We do," Pip responded. "And we have one here, very interested in your hestrs," she said smiling.

"Well then, it looks like we have a deal," Alvis said grinning.

I tried to hide my smile. Pip was winning over every single elder. The only remaining three were Jodis, Emla, and Runa. Pip knew she already had all three of them.

She turned to Jodis, smiling, "you must be Jodis?"

Jodis looked surprised, "How did you know?"

"Agnarr told me you are their head teacher. I was a teacher back on Earth. Like recognizes like," she said laughing. "Do you like teaching the young orklings?"

"I love it, though it would be great if we had someone who was willing to step in and teach the orklings about human ways," Jodis responded, looking hopeful.

"I am not going to lie, Jodis. I am happy to no longer be teaching. But once I gain my footing, I would consider stepping in to provide education on human customs—especially considering we will likely have many half-orkin young in the coming years," Pip said thoughtfully.

At this, Magna didn't even bother to disguise his scoff. Piper's eyes whipped back to him.

"You know, you can leave, right?" she said.

Magna's eyes narrowed, "I'm an elder."

"Yes, and we clearly have the support of the majority of the elders in our decision to integrate the human females into the tribe, your voice is unnecessary if you are going to continue to fight against a decision that has already been made," Piper said quietly. "As it stands, we have eight elders in support of the integration of the humans and one against.

We have, what would be called in my world, a super majority. So you can see yourself out if you don't wish to be part of a meaningful conversation about how that is going to happen."

"And how do you know you have eight to one?" Magna said, attempting to look smug.

Pip looked at the two remaining elders, Emla and Runa.

"We have human cooks and healers, you good with us joining Fýrifírar?" she said in a dangerously casual tone.

Both females nodded silently.

Piper looked back to Magna, "See, you aren't really needed here. You can either sit in silence or leave."

Magna slowly stood, and walked silently toward the door, pushing it open and leaving the meeting. All eyes swiveled back to Piper.

"Well, now that we have him taken care of, can we start making an actual plan?" she said, trying, but failing to hide her satisfied grin.

CHAPTER 12

PIPER

The rest of the meeting focused on how best to introduce the human women to the tribe. We decided on a formal dinner in one week's time. This would give the humans enough time to prepare to meet the tribe officially, and give the tribe enough time to put their best foot forward for the human women. It would be an *event* for all of those involved. My role was to prepare the human women—ensuring they would be ready to be perceived as possible mates by all eligible males. For some of the females, like Billie, this would require no work whatsoever. For others, this was going to be a significant event. We went back and forth on the details for what felt like hours before I finally grabbed Agnarr's thigh. I was emotionally spent.

"Can we continue this conversation tomorrow?" Agnarr asked brusquely, while one of the elders was in the middle of speaking.

All eyes pivoted to Agnarr.

"Piper has had an exceptionally draining dagr, I would like to take her home and care for her," he said, looking at me.

Astrid looked at me and nodded, "Yes, let's reconvene tomorrow morning, after the first meal," she said.

"That sounds wonderful," I said, trying to keep the emotion out of my voice.

I was exhausted and wanted to curl up in a ball next to Agnarr. As the meeting was adjourned, I grabbed Agnarr's hand, heading toward the double doors of the longhouse. Jarlin Astrid caught up with us and grabbed my hand, pulling me to her.

"You did well," she whispered in my ear. "Don't stop holding the line for the humans." Then she walked to the door as if nothing had occurred.

Agnarr looked at me with a question in his gaze.

"Don't worry about it. I need food. And sleep," I said, desperate to get back to his room. We exited the longhouse and once we were out of view of the other elders, Agnarr scooped me up and carried me.

"Agnarr, for the hundredth time I can walk!" I exclaimed.

"You are exhausted, are you not?" he asked, breathing in the scent of my hair.

"I'm dying. I need food and sleep," I said.

"Then that is what you shall have," he said, striding confidently toward his room.

We reached our destination and he still didn't let me down. He opened the door with one hand, while still holding me against his chest. Agnarr gently deposited me on one of the chairs near the fireplace while he scurried around.

It wasn't long before there was a roaring fire in the fireplace, lighting up the room and providing warmth. I sat, staring at the fire, unthinking, happy to just be comfortable. It *had* been a long day.

"Our evening meal should be here soon," he responded, "how are you feeling?"

"Honestly?" I said. And then I just couldn't anymore. I started sobbing. My whole body was wracked with the force of my tears. I covered my face with my hands, trying to hide the tears leaking from my eyes.

Agnarr closed the distance between us in seconds. He was on his knees in front of me, stroking my hair and murmuring comforting words as I cried. I took my hands from my face and wrapped them around his neck as I continued to unload the emotional turmoil from the day.

"What is it, Pip?" he asked urgently as he stroked my hair and my arms.

"Today was just a lot. I am capable—more than capable—of defending myself and others with the ferocity necessary, but it comes at a cost. I am exhausted. Having to prove our worth to the elders took every ounce of energy I have," I explained.

"Oh, Pip," Agnarr took me from my seat and gathered me into his strong arms, wrapping me up. "You did so good today, every single elder was impressed by you, even Magna," he said gently while peppering kisses over the side of my face.

At this, I simply cried harder, knowing I had done my very best for the other humans, but was so tired of having to defend our place here. Agnarr held me, letting me cry myself out in his arms. The mental burden of the day weighed heavily on me and I knew I needed to get up and face another day of it. It was my job to make sure these women were comfortable here and as much as I wanted to meet it head-on, I was exhausted. I cried quietly as Agnarr stroked my hair.

There was a quiet knock at the door, which Agnarr left unanswered, as he continued to hold me. I continued to cry, but as my crying subsided, Agnarr shifted, sitting me upright.

"Are you ready to eat?" he asked.

"Is there food?"

"Já." He placed me in one of the chairs by the fire before opening the door to his room.

He returned with a literal mountain of food on a tray. He set it on the low table between the chairs, allowing me to look at what was available. There was a giant pile of braised meat in gravy, next to what looked similar to roasted carrots and turnips. The other side of the tray featured what looked to be mashed potatoes, but I could only hope.

"This looks delicious," I said, giving him a watery smile.

Agnarr set about making a plate for me, giving me a little bit of everything. It was far more than I would be able to eat, again, but I appreciated his desire to feed me. He handed me a plate and a fork, before serving himself. I took a bite of the meat and gravy, moaning aloud. I didn't realize how much my body needed sustenance.

"Good?" Agnarr asked.

"Very good," I responded, mouth full of food.

I quickly sampled the vegetables and the mashed potato-looking dish, discovering it was all wonderfully seasoned. When I was emotionally overwhelmed I tended to forget that real food would do wonders in making me feel whole again. Each bite brought my anxiety down a level. As I filled my belly, I felt myself calm.

I was okay. The meeting had gone well. The human women would be cared for. I could take a breath and take care of myself. I continued to shovel food into my mouth as Agnarr ate, patiently watching me.

"Better?" he asked as I finished the majority of the food on my plate.

"Yes. I was worried. So worried. I feel like I can take a

deep breath for the first time," I said honestly. "Being assertive puts a huge strain on me, even if I know I can make it appear as though I can take on the entire room."

"You did take on the entire room," Agnarr said quietly.

I sighed. I knew I had the spine. I just didn't know if I had the stamina.

"I know—I'm just exhausted after the fact. I will continue to fight but I will pay the price."

AGNARR

Piper looked as if she would pass out at any moment. I would've loved to offer her a bath, but we were still in my old room and I knew she didn't have the energy to head to the saunas. She'd finished eating and was staring into the flickering flames with a dazed look on her face. Pip had been such a commanding presence in the meeting, taking charge of the room without hesitation. I was going to have to learn to see the small signs of strain when we were in meetings and public events. I had no idea she was on the brink of tears when we left the building. I was immensely proud of her. I vowed to myself to be her safe place to land after big days like this.

I headed to the restroom and returned with a wet cloth. Without comment, I wiped away the dried tears from Pip's face, before gently kissing her. She sighed into me.

"Shall we go to bed?" I asked.

"Yes, please," she said, standing.

She sat on the bed to pull off her boots and leggings, before removing her tunic. I drank in the sight of her naked body, nipples pebbled in the cold air but shut down that part of my mind. She needed rest. I took her clothes and dumped them in the laundry basket by the door, as she crawled into bed. I disrobed and joined her, pulling her to me. Instead of spooning, we lay facing each other.

"Who does the laundry?" she asked sleepily.

"Part of the kitchen team," I responded, running my finger softly across her bottom lip. "There is a whole laundry facility"

"Well, that seems nice..." she said drifting off, her eyes fluttering closed.

I stroked her hair and watched her fall asleep. She started to softly snore almost immediately. I wasn't nearly as tired as she was. She really ran the show during the meeting today. I was in awe of her presence. I wondered what she must have been like as a teacher. I could imagine her controlling a room of adolescent orkin with ease. I had so many questions about what she'd overcome to be such a resilient little thing, but I just watched her sleep for a while.

Eventually, I got out of bed, turned down the lamps, and added another log to the fire. I rejoined her in bed and pulled her toward me.

She murmured in her sleep, "Agnarr?"

"I'm here, rest, sweet Pip."

She snuggled into my side and returned to snoring. I wanted to give her everything. I thought of what I could do to make life easier for my Pip. We needed to get a move into our new home. I wanted her to come back to her own home each day—maybe we could even make an office just for her. I would need to speak to Osif about the plans for our house amongst the furutré. I would also speak to Bram about setting up a meetings for Pip with some of the merchants in town for bedding and furniture and all the comforts of home. Pip would want for nothing.

* * *

THE ELDERS FILED in for the council meeting the next morning. As we all took our seats, Astrid spoke.

"I'm surprised to see you back, Elder Magna," she said crisply.

"I thought I would return to you with some numbers," he responded.

"Oh, please, do share," Astrid said, resting her chin on fists.

"I have thirty orkin with me, unwilling to accept the human females," he said coldly.

"And of those thirty, how many of them are of mating age?" Astrid asked.

"Fifteen."

"And how many of your sons?"

"One," Magna responded, attempting to hold his ground.

"So even with the thirty orkin you managed to convince of your outdated ideas, you were only able to convince *one* of your three sons?" Astrid replied, shocked.

At this Magna looked at his lap, "The other two are interested in finding a mate. They think a human female might be their only hope," he said.

"Ah," Astrid said knowingly. "And what do you and the thirty orkin you've collected plan to do?"

"Leave," Magna said bluntly.

"And go where?" Piper interjected.

"We were thinking the Snaerfírar tribe in the north might not be so willing to accept weak humans," Magna sneered.

"So not only are you a misogynist, you clearly have trouble listening. You've already discussed with Jarl Agnarr that the Snaerfírar tribe has accepted human women and has the half-orc offspring to prove it," Pip purred.

"Perhaps you'd have better luck with the Vátrfírar tribe in the south," I said, keeping my eyes on Piper. After yesterday, I didn't want her to overexert herself fighting all the battles for the human women.

"You're certain the Snaerfírar tribe was accepting of human women?" Magna grumbled.

"Steve seemed very happy and beloved in his tribe. He held a position of trust and was treated as equal. So, yeah, we're pretty certain," Pip said, seemingly unruffled.

Magna shifted in his seat, clearly uncomfortable with the news he'd just received.

"Well, it is your choice, Magna. Are you going to take your followers and head to Vátrfírar or are you going to stay and respect the human women?" Astrid questioned.

"I will have to discuss with those with me. We all had agreed to head to Snaerfírar. This... changes things," he said gruffly.

"Well, feel free to do so. However, would you please send us your eldest son as your replacement? We want to move forward with our plans," Astrid asked.

"How did you know my eldest was in support of the human women?" he huffed.

"How old is Skaard?" Astrid asked.

"Thirty-three árs."

"And still no mate?"

"No."

"And how old is Iric?"

"Twenty-eight árs."

"Ozur?"

"Twenty-two árs."

"So let me guess," Astrid said calmly, "Skaard and Iric want to stay, with hopes of finding a human mate. It was only Ozur, your youngest, that you were able to convince of the 'weakness' of human females?"

Magna looked dumbstruck, blinking rapidly.

"Alright, go speak with your followers and form a plan.

Please send us either Skaard or Iric in your stead," Astrid said, clearly bored of Magna.

"Also, as you are making your plans, please take into consideration that we won't be allowing you to take any of our hestrs. Any of the traveling you do will have to take place on foot," Alvis interjected.

Magna rose, looking disgusted at the elders at the table, "We will never retain our status as a strong okin race if we are willing to breed with these weak pathetic females," he sneered.

It was happening before I could stop it, Pip was out of her seat so quickly that the chair toppled over behind her. She reached Magna in three strides, hauled back, and slapped him directly across the mouth. It was only Magna's moment of shock that saved Pip. I stood and placed myself behind her, hand around her waist.

"You can go," I said firmly.

Magna hesitated, looking as if he actually considered taking me on, but stepped back in defeat.

"I shall send Skaard," Magna said as he walked out, not bothering to look back.

CHAPTER 13

PIPER

As I returned to my seat I tried to compose myself. I'd just slapped an elder across the face. That was probably not the best choice. But I couldn't take Magna referring to us as *weak* humans anymore. Agnarr's unwavering support helped comfort me, but I still felt ill at ease as I looked around the table at the other elders. I was expecting looks of judgment or reproach, but all of the elders were looking at me with support and perhaps, sympathy?

"I'm sorry you had to experience Magna," Emla started.

"He's of an older perspective," Jodis explained. "It is probably for the best that he is no longer part of the discussions."

"His age doesn't permit him to treat the humans with such disrespect. It's going to bode well for us that he is being replaced by Skaard. He's of a much different mindset," Astrid stated.

"Well, as we wait for Skaard to join us, can we continue in preparation for the integration of the humans?" I asked.

"Yes, let's continue," Runa said eagerly.

We were planning a formal dinner to introduce the humans, having kept them isolated for over a week. I had breakfast with them this morning and I could tell they were feeling cooped up, even if they were still hesitant about meeting the rest of the orkin.

"We can have the cooks plan an elaborate meal," Runa returned to the conversation.

"That isn't necessary, I promise you, they have been impressed with the food they have been provided thus far, as have I," I said grinning.

Runa's withered cheeks darkened with a blush, "My thanks, Jarlin Piper."

"We will be happy with whatever you prepare. Back in the States, most cities don't eat communally. Women cook for themselves, their partners, and their families most nights. Things have changed over time, but most women are expected to be the cook in the family. I think all of these women are grateful for a home-cooked meal that they didn't have to make," I explained.

Agnarr stroked my thigh under the table, I was learning this was his way of checking in on me. I grasped his hand, giving it a quick squeeze to let him know I was just fine.

"Would it be appropriate to have some of our younger orklings perform a song to welcome the women?" Jodis asked quietly.

"That would be lovely."

"They could also help with decorating the longhouse to make it a bit more festive," she said, sounding slightly more confident.

"That sounds excellent," Agnarr said, hand still on my thigh.

"Is there anything else we can do to make the event more festive?" Astrid asked.

AGNARR'S JARLIN

I thought about it for a bit, "Do orcs dance?" I asked.

The room erupted in laughter, I wasn't sure if that was a firm no or a firm yes. Seeing the confused look on my face, Agnarr leaned in to explain.

"Já, we love to dance. There is music and dancing after every newly mated pair's announcement. You and I missed out on that tradition by choosing each other in Niflfýri," he said softly, "Usually there is a big celebration when Elska mates—or any mates—choose each other."

"Ah, I see," I said. "Well then, heck yes to music and dancing!"

The elders looked a little puzzled at my language but seemed to understand my agreement. It was at this moment that a handsome orc, looking to be about Agnarr's age, walked into the longhouse and sat down in Magna's seat, without commentary. All the elders looked at him as if waiting for him to speak.

"Hello," he said, his voice cracking. He cleared his throat and tried again, "Hello, I am apparently the new elder representing the smiths, I'm Skaard."

Skaard looked a little nervous being at the elders' table, and I wanted to assure him that he was welcome, based on what Magna had said. "Skaard, what are your feelings about the human women joining the tribe?"

"I think it is our duty to take in any refugees, regardless of what they can offer the tribe. This is obviously something my father and I disagree on," Skaard said, shifting in his seat uncomfortably.

"I appreciate your acceptance and your support, especially given what it cost you personally," I said.

"Thank you, Jarlin Piper, for acknowledging the cost. My family has been torn apart by this. My youngest brother is planning to leave with my father within the next viká. I can't bear to think how our mother would handle this. Thankfully, she isn't here to see all of this ugliness," he explained solemnly.

"I am glad to have you with us, Skaard. I hope you are able to find a mate through this process, human or otherwise," I said.

Skaard gave me the briefest of smiles, before forging forward, "I am sure I interrupted a conversation, please continue."

"Actually, I think we were just finishing," I said, looking around the table. "A celebration and formal introduction of the human women in one week?"

"Já, one vika," Astrid said.

"You've forgotten something," Bram piped up.

I looked at him in surprise, "Oh?"

"Já. I assume the humans will want to look their very best for this occasion?" he asked.

"Yes, I suppose that is true," I agreed.

"I would be willing to send some of the tailors to help dress the females. Free of charge, of course," he said genially.

"That would be lovely, Bram. Truly, the human women will appreciate it beyond measure. I know most of them will have never had a custom-made gown," I said.

"I am happy that our community will be able to provide for them," he responded.

"Well, if that settles all of the plans, I would like to inform them of the tribe's decision," I said.

"Yes, yes, by all means," Astrid said. "Meeting adjourned, everyone off to work on their own preparations for the celebration," she directed.

I stood and looked at Agnarr. He stood as well but didn't grasp my hand.

"I have some matters to attend to with Elder Osif, are you alright to meet with the humans on your own?" he asked.

"Of course," I murmured, knowing full well that my intention was to run to them with the news.

"Perfect," he said, before pulling me into a rough embrace.

AGNARR

I watched as Piper left the longhouse before approaching Osif. He remained, as if he knew I would want to speak with him. When it was just the two of us in the longhouse I asked, "What plans have you made for our new home?"

"Jarlin Piper has requested that I keep those secret. I will honor her request," he said, tone serious.

"Can I add an additional request?" I asked.

"So long as it doesn't interfere with Jarlin Piper's wishes, I am happy to accommodate yours."

"Can we dedicate a space for Jarlin Piper, alone? A space for her to meet with other human females, a space where she feels comfortable?" I asked.

"Your living space is plenty large for us to devote part of it to meeting with the humans, I will adjust accordingly," Osif said.

"Please keep this from Piper. I want to surprise her with how we've outfitted our home," I explained.

"Of course," Osif agreed, bowing to me, out of practice.

"Please—Piper views you as an equal, as do I. Never feel the need to bow to my leadership," I said, before turning to leave the longhouse.

PIPER

After the meeting with the elders, I was exhausted. I wanted a nap and an iced latte, but I knew I needed to meet with the women. I gave Agnarr a brief kiss, before heading to Emla's cabin—their safe space. As I approached the cabin, I squared my shoulders, ready for another intense meeting. I opened the door and everyone inside went silent—great. Eleven sets of human eyeballs were on me. *Teacher mode activated.*

"Hi, y'all," I said enthusiastically.

Students always assumed I was from the South because of my use of the term 'y'all' when really, I was just trying to be inclusive. I slipped into it without realizing it.

"Hi!" Billie said enthusiastically.

Thank the universe for Billie, she was happy to be here and I needed it.

"So, I am guessing you are waiting on some news?" I asked.

All of the human women looked expectantly at me. No pressure.

"So, the good news is, I have no bad news," I said smiling, "Jarlin Astrid, Agnarr, and I have managed to convince the elders to accept the human women with no expectation. There is no expectation that you take a mate, or that you even look for a mate. They are willing to integrate you into the tribe, as long as you are willing to share the burden of keeping the tribe going."

"What do you mean, 'share the burden?'" Olivia asked.

"I'm actually glad it was you that asked, Liv," I said. "They want us to use our skills and abilities to help the tribe. They were very interested in having an animal healer amongst the human women. As soon as you are comfortable, I will introduce you to Alvis, the keeper of the hestrs."

"Ooh, I would love that," Liv responded.

"So, there are a ton of different ways that everyone can contribute, based on their skills and abilities. Our willingness to do so has gained us equal standing amongst the orkin," I explained. "Well that, and might have accidentally slapped an elder," I said somewhat self-deprecatingly.

"You what?" Eleanor gasped.

"Well, there was one elder with a handful of followers that don't want to see human women integrated into the tribe. He thinks we are weak and will produce weak offspring. He kept going on about it, even though none of the other elders agreed with him and I got to a point where I couldn't take his bullshit anymore, so I slapped him. Whoops?" I said, shrugging.

Several of the women started laughing, while others looked shocked.

"Um, what happened to the elder you slapped?" Zoey asked.

"He and his followers are choosing to leave the tribe."

"Is Jarlin Astrid upset by this?" Diedre asked, looking shocked.

"Honestly, she has been 100% supportive. She is ready to step down and she has shown nothing but support for me and Agnarr. I don't think she even cares," I explained.

"We really appreciate you fighting for us," Gemma said. "I know with your anxiety that can't have been easy."

I let out a sigh and unclenched, I was in a safe space, "It was not easy. I can be a fierce advocate when I need to be, but I am mentally exhausted afterward. I need a nap and a shot," I said with a laugh.

"Come, sit," Billie said, offering me a chair.

I melted into the chair, trying to release some of the tension I'd felt with the elders. I was here with my sisters, and they all seemed to be concerned for me first and foremost. I was ready to become a puddle of skin, and all of the women were so supportive. I had to at least explain the plan to them.

"Okay, so we have decided that in a week's time, y'all will be introduced and integrated into the tribe. It will be a festive event with dancing and a feast, all of the elders are excited about it."

All of the women started to talk amongst each other at this announcement and I stayed silent, giving them time to process together. Most of the women were excited, talking about what they would wear and what it would be like to have time with the orkin. Others were talking quietly about being scared to take on a mate and meet the males. I felt out of my element. I didn't know what I could do to help make them more comfortable. I wanted to be everywhere, offering support, but I could only keep track of so many conversations. I ended up joining a conversation with Zoey and Lucy. They were both hesitant to meet the male orkin, given their past. Zoey had severe PTSD from her former partner and her time in the military and Lucy was a cancer survivor, having had a double mastectomy. Neither of them was emotionally prepared to take on a mate.

I listened patiently as Zoey and Lucy aired their concerns to me. I could understand their hesitation.

"This is a big step," I said gently. "No one should feel pressured into anything they're not ready for."

Zoey nodded, her expression grim. "I don't know if I'll ever be ready. The thought of being intimate again...it terrifies me." She wrapped her arms around herself, as if for protection.

"Me too," said Lucy quietly. "I'm scared of letting someone get close again."

My heart ached for them. I wished I could take away their pain and fear surrounding intimacy.

"The right partner won't push you into anything," I reassured. " And there's no set timeline. You can take all the time you need."

Zoey managed a small smile. "Thanks. I needed to hear that."

"Me too," Lucy agreed. "It helps to talk about it."

I hugged them both, hoping they understood that they

weren't alone. No matter what happened, I would be there for them.

Trauma bonding was no joke. We all experienced the same loss of purpose, livelihood, family, etcetera. Though we came from different backgrounds, we understood each other's pain. I was scared to be something other than being a teacher—it was all I knew. We were all stuck in this messed up situation, yet they were ready to accept me outside of my role as a teacher—something I'd never been used to. I wanted to be more than a high school teacher for the Fýrifírar tribe. I had to be in order to be jarlin.

As I looked around, I noticed all the women in hand-me-down, ill-fitting orkin clothing and realized I'd forgotten to share Bram's offer.

I called out to the group, "I forgot to share part of the agreement. Bram, the orc that represents the merchants, has offered to send us one of the tailors from the tribe to custom-make our outfits for the celebration."

A cheer erupted from the group. I continued to feel my walls come down with these women. I needed to get to know each of them and I didn't want my anxiety to get in the way. I had few friends back on Earth. I always hesitated to reach out—feeling I was a bother. This would not work for me as jarlın. I was going to have to get comfortable reaching out to each woman regularly. I would have to figure out a way to touch base with each woman in a way that felt natural and comfortable for me. I rolled that around in my head as the women chatted about what they would wear to the welcome celebration. I was definitely going to have to shift gears mentally.

I was lost in thought when my stomach reminded me that breakfast had been long ago. As much as I would have enjoyed having a meal with the other women, I was socially done for the day. I wanted to head back to Agnarr's room, hoping that I'd find him there. I started thinking of his thick muscled thighs and felt my mouth water at the thought. Holy hell, I had never wanted a man the way I wanted Agnarr. I looked around to see all of the women talking amongst themselves. I quietly stood and snuck out the door as the women continued to discuss their ideas for what they would wear to the celebration. None of them noticed me go. I skipped in victory toward Agnarr's room.

I felt lighter than I had in two days. Astrid was happy, the elders were happy, and the humans were happy. I could breathe a sigh of relief. I quickly reached Agnarr's room to find it empty. It was still a bit early for the midday meal—nothing had been delivered yet. With all of our meetings, this was our only alone time. The mating frenzy was still in full effect and I needed my orc.

CHAPTER 14

AGNARR

I met with Osif and followed up with Astrid while Pip met with the human women. Everyone was on the same page. I even spoke with Bram before I headed to my room and agreed that the tailors would visit the humans the following dagr. I wanted my room, my bed. The meeting with the elders had been exhausting. I'd been ready to physically fight Magna after Pip slapped him. Luckily, he saw he was outnumbered and chose to exit. I appreciated his decency in that—if nothing else. The addition of Skaard would make our meetings run much more smoothly. I approached my room, seeing the midday meal had yet to be delivered. Maybe I could take a nap before Piper joined me.

I opened the door to my room to find Piper asleep in my bed, arms wrapped around my pillow. I headed to my toilet and stripped, wiping myself down with a wet cloth and soap. Perhaps Pip and I could 'spoon' for a bit before the midday meal was delivered. I left my washroom and crawled into bed with Piper, wrapping my much larger body around hers. I stroked along her hip and the curve of her ass, trying to keep myself under control. Pip needed sleep. I settled myself around her only to be surprised by her husky voice.

"I've been waiting for you," she breathed, reaching her arm back and grabbing my braid with her hand.

"You weren't asleep!" I gasped.

"Not even a little bit," she chuckled.

"So, you took off all your clothes and got into bed because..." I trailed off.

"Because I've been thinking about riding your magnificent cock since this morning?" she said, unabashedly grinding her ass into my quickly growing erection.

I flipped her so we were face-to-face, "I missed you," I breathed, stroking her cheek.

She took my hand in hers, "Do we have the time?" she asked.

"They'll leave the midday meal at the door and I don't have anything else scheduled for today, so we have all the time. Unless you have meetings?" I continued to stroke down her jawline, hungry to kiss her soft lips.

"No plans," she took my face with her hands pulling me into a fierce kiss. She nibbled and sucked at my lower lip until I opened for her. She slid her tongue in exploring me, lovingly stroking her tongue along each tusk, before licking along my ridged tongue. "Have I told you how much I love these?"

"Love what?" I asked, confused.

"Your tusks. I love the feel of them when we kiss, I love the press of them as you nip down my body. I love feeling them on my thighs as you lick me," she said, stroking her hand languidly up and down my spine, tracing my mating marks with her fingers.

I blushed a deep green. My tusks were just my tusks. Part

of me. I could understand her love of my cock and my muscles, but my tusks? That was new.

"Well, I shall make sure you feel them every time I kiss or lick you," I responded, pulling her in for another kiss. Perhaps it was her lack of tusks that made mine seem so appealing. I found her tiny white tuskless teeth to be perfect, especially when she was doing her damndest to get my entire cock down her throat. I groaned into our kiss at the thought.

Pip pulled away, "Did you think of something, or am I that good of a kisser?" she teased.

"You are an amazing kisser," I said, in between peppering her cheeks and tiny nose with kisses, "but I will admit, I thought of your soft mouth wrapped around my cock."

Pips, eyes brightened. She said nothing as she started to plant soft open-mouthed kisses down my neck, stopping to drag her tongue along my collarbone. My fists clutched the sheets beneath me, determined not to interrupt her exploration. She continued to press kisses down my chest and torso, licking down one hip bone and then the other causing me to press my face into the pillow to stifle a growl. She lifted her head slightly and I could feel her breath on my cock. It took all of my power not to fist her hair and guide her lips down onto me. This would *always* be her choice. Yet as she dragged her tongue from the base of my cock to the tip, I couldn't stop myself from thrusting upward. She chuckled at my clear want and then finally wrapped her lips around me, pulling me into her warm mouth. She fisted the base, encircling my knot, before she began to pump me with her mouth and hand in a steady rhythm. My eyes rolled back as I felt her smooth tongue drag along the underside of my shaft, all while she continued to pump my knot. She steadily bobbed her fist and mouth up and down, unraveling me with each rhythmic motion.

"I—I won't last much longer at this rate," I whispered hoarsely.

Pip paused her movement and popped her mouth off me. She looked at me curiously, almost assessing.

"You know, there's something I've always wanted to do, but was never able to with any of my partners."

"Oh?" I rasped, still very aware of the proximity of her mouth to my cock.

"I've never had sex up against a wall. I've always wanted to, but never had a partner that could lift—" I cut her off mid-sentence, reaching down and pulling her up the length of my body, closing the distance between us.

I rolled out of bed and took her with me, carrying her to the closest wall and pinning her to it with my much larger frame. She wrapped her legs around my waist, trapping my cock between us before I dipped low for another kiss. The taste of my cock on her tongue only drove my need higher. I ground my hips into hers as she pulled back, gasping for air.

PIPER

I pressed my palms to Agnarr's muscled chest, trying to steady myself. I had my legs wrapped around him as he held me against the wall.

"You've never? You've... Never?" he breathed, reverently stroking his hands up and down my sides, pausing to slide a teasing finger under the swell of my breasts.

"No, they told me I was too heavy—or they'd make it a few thrusts but be unable to continue," I said breathlessly, very aware he was holding me against the wall with almost no effort.

Agnarr growled deep in his throat before shifting his hands to grab my ass and pulling me up higher. He leaned down, dragging a textured tongue along my puckered nipple, before sucking it into his mouth. My hands went to his hair, slipping into his unraveling braid.

Agnarr switched breasts, pulling my other nipple into his mouth, and I couldn't take it anymore. Every nerve ending was on fire and I needed him inside me before I exploded with want. My clit was throbbing and angry at the attention my nipples were getting.

"I need you inside me. Now. Right now," I said, shamelessly grinding my mound against his cock.

Agnarr's pupils blew out with lust as he reached down and dragged the tip of his cock against my wet slit.

"You're sure you want me like this?" he asked, cock poised at my entrance.

"Gods, yes," I hissed, trying to move my hips onto the head of his cock. I tried to move to take him, but I couldn't. He had me pinned against the rough fututre wall. I was trapped by his arms and his hips, at his mercy.

"You're sure?" he rasped. "Because I can't go easy on you, I want you too badly."

"I want all of you, Agnarr. I never want you to hold back," I gasped.

Agnarr lined up the head of his cock and plunged into me. I gasped at the overwhelming but welcome feel of his thickness. Though we'd now fucked countless times, he always stretched me to the limit. I tried to relax to allow him to fully settle into me, though my body was screaming *yes* and *too much* simultaneously. Pinned against the wall, I could do nothing but accept his thrusts into me. I spread my hips wider with his large hands on my ass. I wanted all of him. Each thrust of his ridged and braided cock dragged across my sensitive g-spot, causing me to quickly unravel. His knot pressed against every inch of me and I was hanging on by a thread. I had always wanted to be taken roughly against a wall and had always been disappointed.

Agnarr could never disappoint. He rutted into me at a steady pace. Each drag of his cock opened me up further and further, my walls fluttering against the braided ridges of him. He shifted me slightly, pulling me wider and thrusting faster. Suddenly, his one hand left my ass cheek. He grabbed my chin and pulled it up causing me to lock eyes with him.

"I want to look you in the eye as you come around my cock," he growled.

Oh fuck. I loved bossy Agnarr almost as much as I loved caring, considerate Agnarr. Being eye-to-eye as he thrust into me was more than I'd ever experienced. There was no imagining that this didn't happen. This wasn't a tryst in the supply closet at Christian camp that I would be shamed for later. This was a complete claiming. Agnarr's eyes never left mine as he ratcheted up the pace, one hand easily supporting my weight, the other firmly holding my jaw. I was at his mercy and he was relentless, pummeling into me as I gasped for air.

"This—this is what I've always wanted, but never felt I could ask for," I gasped.

"Já, and what's that?" he asked, never changing his pace.

"I wanted," I gasped for air, "I wanted a partner that would fuck me like he owned me."

Agnarr's eyes never left mine, instead pulling me to him for a plundering kiss. I tightened my fingers in his hair. His lips on mine, his hips snapping against me, his cock as deep as my body would allow.

"This cunt is mine, Piper. No one else's," he growled, before releasing my chin. "Watch, watch how well your cunt takes my cock."

I looked down to see him sliding in and out of me obscenely. No one had ever given me permission to enjoy sex this much and it was enough to undo me. Watching his textured, knotted, green cock slip in and out of me, glistening with my own arousal was unspeakably hot. My breath caught in my throat as I clenched down around his magnificent length, coming, and coming, and coming. I shuddered as pleasure coiled through me.

"Oh fuck, Agnarr. Oh, fuck me!"

" I *am* fucking you," he growled.

"I'm coming," I panted.

I reached the end of my climax and slumped against the wall, relying completely on Agnarr to hold me in place. Agnarr slid his arms from my ass to my waist, guiding me back to his bed, all while still thick and throbbing inside of me. He splayed me out on his bed, never pulling out. I used the last of my energy to wrap my legs around his waist. It was as if watching me come had spurred Agnarr on even more. He kissed every inch of exposed skin. He pulled one nipple into his warm mouth, flicking his tongue against it. I was spent, thinking there was no way I could crest another peak, but he wasn't done with me.

Agnarr sawed in and out of me, his hands and tongue everywhere. It was all I could do to remember to breathe. My vision was hazy with pleasure. I didn't think I had another climax in me, but Agnarr's forceful pounding and thumbs on my nipples were enough to convince my body otherwise. It wasn't long before I felt myself starting to uncoil underneath him. He grabbed my chin, pausing his thrusting.

"Come with me, Pip," he growled.

"I don't know if I can," I gasped.

"You can and you will."

He continued to slide in and out of me while he nipped and sucked at my nipples. It had only been a short time with Agnarr, but he knew that sucking my nipples ratcheted everything for me. The feeling of suction on my nipple zipped straight to my clit that was being massaged by Agnarr's knot every time he hammered into me.

It was too much! Too much!

I thrashed my head from side to side as he took me. He wanted another orgasm from me and wasn't going to stop until he'd gotten one. He slipped his hand between us and found my swollen clit. He circled it slowly all while keeping up his pace, before pressing down on it with the pad of his thumb. My crest came with a shock and I dug my nails into his shoulders, clenching my legs around him. All that came out of me was an unintelligible scream. I panted and grasped onto him, clinging to him as I came undone.

As Agnarr's thrusts became more harried and uneven I knew he was close. I arched my hips up to meet each thrust. He grasped me tighter, burying his face in the soft skin where my shoulder met my neck, I felt the kick of his release and the clamp down on my neck at the same time and gasped at the sensations. My mind short-circuited on the pleasure-pain of his cum filling me while his tusks were at my neck. Agnarr ruined me for any other man. It would always be Agnarr. He collapsed atop me, breathing heavily. I loved the weight of him pressing into me, listening to both of our heart rates slow as we came down from the high of our orgasms. I languidly stroked up and down Agnarr's sides as his breathing slowed.

Agnarr propped himself up on his elbows to look at me, and instead of the satisfied love-drunk expression I was expecting, I was met with a look of horror.

"What—what's wrong?" I asked, touching his cheek.

"I've marked you... Everywhere. I've hurt you," he said, as he assessed my body beneath him, face filled with shame.

I looked down and sure enough, there were hickeys on my boobs and my torso. There would most definitely be marks on my neck and likely my thighs as well. Agnarr continued to look at me as if he had committed a crime.

"Agnarr, look at me," I said, trying to pull his eyes away from the marks he'd left.

I pulled his chin so we were eye-to-eye.

"What did I ask for?" I asked.

"What?" he said, clearly confused.

"What did I ask you to do? Do you remember?" I prompted

I could see the wheels in his head churning, "Um, you asked me to fuck me like I owned you?" he said, clearly uncertain.

"Yes. That's exactly what I asked for. I *like* it when you manhandle me. I *love it* when you leave marks on me. My pussy being sore from being eviscerated by your monster cock reminds me of every moment we shared together. And it makes me want to do it again," I said slowly and clearly.

Agnarr's eyebrows raised so high it was almost comical, "But what will you tell the other women when they see the marks?"

"I'll tell them that the jarl fucked me so good, I can barely walk," I said grinning at his confusion.

Agnarr looked even more horrified, "I don't want to harm you!"

I couldn't help myself, I started full-blown cackling. This poor adorable orc thought he was abusing me when all he'd done was fuck me boneless. As I continued to laugh, Agnarr's confusion turned to frustration.

"Will you please explain this human custom I am clearly misunderstanding?" he said gruffly.

"Why don't we clean up and then we can talk a little about human mating customs."

Agnarr slid out of me with an audible squelch before heading to the washroom. After a few minutes, he returned with a warm washcloth and carefully cleaned me up before tossing the washcloth aside. He climbed into bed, facing me, stroking my jawline.

"Okay, so. The idea of being fucked so good that you can't walk is *appealing* to many human women," I explained, trying not to sound condescending.

"So, you want me to fuck you so hard that it's uncomfortable to walk the next day?" he asked, clearly confused.

"Yep. Every step I take will remind me of our time together."

"But it hurts?"

"I mean, sure, a little. I would never let it get to a point where it was like, oh god I need a doctor hurt," I explained. "Your cock is the biggest I've ever taken, if you fuck me like you own me, I am bound to be a little sore."

"And you still want to do this?" he asked, looking at me warily.

"Absolutely. I love being stuffed full with your giant cock," I grinned.

Agnarr slapped a hand across my mouth, as if afraid someone would hear. I removed his fingers gently and pulled him into a kiss. He was gentle and oh so tender, as if afraid he'd break me.

"I've been with men who have been afraid to express their wants, or felt shame about their needs. I'm not interested in that. If you want to bend me over and fuck me while I am in the middle of cooking dinner, I am absolutely here for it," I breathed. "I never want to feel my sexuality confined again, and that extends to you. If you want something, ask. And we'll discuss how to make sure both our needs are met."

Agnarr took a breath before responding, "So you like it when I am not careful with you?"

"Mmm, very much. I like when you take control. Like when you pulled my hair? That was amazing. I am used to always having to be in control, giving that to you is amazing."

He looked thoughtful, "And I didn't hurt you?" he asked.

"Today? There was a little pinch when you slammed into me, but nothing that was unmanageable."

"And you'd tell me if something was too much?"

"Of course, wouldn't you tell me?"

"You could never be too much for me, sweet Pip."

I melted into him, snuggling closer to his warm chest, "So we're in agreement? You won't hold back and you trust me to tell you if something is too much?"

"Mmm," was all he responded with as he stroked my back up and down.

I closed my eyes and started to drift, the last thought entering my mind being that maybe being abducted by aliens was the best thing that ever happened to me.

CHAPTER 15

PIPER

The next several days were a whirlwind of preparation. I met with the human women daily and made it a point to connect with each of them individually. As I learned more of their stories I learned more about why they were abandoned with the orkin. All of them had either trauma, chronic illnesses, or mental health issues. I'd always been good at meeting people where they were and removing judgment from the equation. It was one of the things that made me such a good teacher. Students felt seen by me and were willing to be vulnerable. This translated easily to relationship-building with the other women and it wasn't long before they all viewed me as a trusted leader and confidant.

I tried to spend as much time with them as I could while also attending council meetings and meetings with Osif about the progress of our new home. Agnarr was just as busy, meeting with the elders, meeting with Astrid, and something secretive that I decided not to pry into. I had so much on my plate that it was easy to ignore whatever Agnarr had in store for me. Osif was splitting his time between working on our home and working on a new space for the human women and I always reminded him to focus on the space for them. I even got him to include a bathing area just for them because I knew so many of them would struggle with bathing communally.

The week passed incredibly quickly and before I knew it, it was time for the welcoming of the humans we'd so carefully planned. We all agreed to get ready together at Emla's cabin, taking turns preening in front of the one full-length mirror. Bram's tailors had pulled out all the stops, making several visits to ensure each woman had a dress they were comfortable in. While all our dresses were definitely of orkin style, they were designed to flatter each of our figures. I was in a gray dress with silver embroidery along the edges. The neck cut dangerously low, exposing what little cleavage I had and the long sleeves belled out with the same intricate embroidery. I felt like a bride at a ren faire. I twisted my hair into what I called a messy crown again and it matched my outfit perfectly.

We'd agreed that the women would all arrive together, so I hadn't seen Agnarr all day. The celebration was to take place in the village square with all of the local shops having a booth and braziers lit to add to the ambiance—and to provide warmth. Though the orkin were used to the snowy season, being outdoors in the cold would provide some difficulty for some of our more slight females. After ensuring that all the women were ready we gathered into a circle in Emla's cabin. All eyes were on me.

"I know this is a lot, but remember, they are ready and excited to meet you. Agnarr, Astrid, and I have put in the work to ensure that you are welcome as you are," I said, trying to soothe any anxiety they felt.

I'd never been part of a sorority in college but I imagined that it must have felt something like this. A sisterhood. We all had each other's backs. We gripped each other's hands tightly.

"Are we ready?" I asked, looking at eleven faces.

Everyone nodded. At this, I ushered them out of Emla's cabin and toward the village center. It was a short distance and it wasn't long before I could see the glowing braziers and the decorative banners that hung in honor of the occasion. We arrived to find the square buzzing with orkin, eating and drinking, ready for a night of celebration. As we approached, the crowd grew quiet. Astrid took it in stride and headed to the small stage that had been erected.

"Orkin of Fýrifírar, I invite you to welcome the newest members of our tribe," she said enthusiastically, gesturing at me and the other women.

To my relief, applause broke out. I knew that Agnarr, Astrid, and the elders had worked hard to ensure that this evening would be a success, having sat in on almost all of the council meetings, but the nervous side of me still anticipated things would go sideways. I watched as the women stepped into the crowd, mingling with the orkin, feeling like an overprotective mother. I was watching each woman like a hawk, ready to step in at any sign of discomfort. Seeing all of the women at ease, I allowed myself to head to the long table set up in the center of the square. It was piled high with food and drink, and I was starving. I hadn't eaten since breakfast. I was in the process of devouring a roasted vegetable pie when I felt a warm breath against my ear.

"You look absolutely delectable."

I jumped and turned to see Agnarr staring down at me, hunger completely unmasked. He was dressed similarly to me, in a gray tunic with silver embroidery and neatly stitched leather pants. Someone had ensured we'd match this evening. He looked as if he would devour me on the spot.

"You look—" I paused, choking on the words, assessing my giant orc. "You look magnificent," I said, dropping the pie and raising my hands to press them against his chest, reveling in the firm muscles underneath his tunic.

"Easy now," he whispered, "we have to make it through this entire evening; you and I are the stars of the show."

"Oh hush, look around you. They might be watching us, but most of them are interested in the other women," I said, looking out at the crowd.

Billie and Ginny were standing, drinks in hand, surrounded by a group of orkin males. I tensed for a minute before I watched the small group erupt in laughter at something Billie had said. Billie was the opposite of me, a delighted extrovert. She was in her element and clearly having a great time finally meeting all of the other orkin. She and Ginny had become fast friends, and I had no reason to worry about them.

My eyes flicked over to all the other human women. Some of them were standing amongst groups of elders having animated conversations, others seated quietly, getting to know the orkin individually. I was pleased to see Zoey, Lucy, and Jodis playing a game that somewhat resembled *duck-duck-goose* with the orklings. I saw Odin shrieking with laughter as he ran around the other orklings, before hiding himself behind Zoey. I breathed a sigh of relief. Of the human women, I was definitely worried about Zoey and Lucy, given their pasts. I would love to see Jodis take them under her wing. Perhaps they'd be a good fit in the classroom.

Agnarr still stood behind me, clearly assessing me for tension. I turned to him.

"I think we could relax for a bit, have you eaten?" I asked.

"No, I wanted to make sure you ate," he mumbled, stroking a thumb across my lower lip.

"You watched me eat!"

"Barely half a vegetable pie," he scoffed.

"Alright, alright, let's get some food," I agreed.

We had deliberately not set a high table, instead opting for several small tables, to allow for more intimate conversation. Agnarr and I got ourselves a sampling of everything that was to offer at the food table—Runa and her team had clearly outdone themselves. We took a seat at an empty table and I was reminded of how hungry I was. I stuffed a large portion of roasted meat in gravy in my mouth and groaned at the taste. I was definitely getting spoiled by communal eating. One of the things I hated the most about living alone on Earth was having to decide what to eat for dinner every night. More often than not, it was something that was frozen and easy. A far cry from the tender, delicately spiced meat I was currently consuming. I continued to attack my meal with enthusiasm until I looked up to find Agnarr staring at me. I swallowed my last bite audibly.

"Aren't you hungry?" I asked, observing his untouched plate.

"Oh I am, but not for food." He licked his lips in a completely obscene way.

I blushed, feeling my clit throb based on Agnarr's look alone, "We'll have plenty of time for that later, you need food—actual food—right now," I admonished, taking another bite of food.

Agnarr grumbled before acquiescing and starting on his own meal. Though he ate with less gusto than I did, I could tell he was enjoying the flavors that Runa and her team had accomplished. As time wore on, and the tribe continued to celebrate, I knew it was time for us to address the crowd.

Astrid, Agnarr, and I had planned this carefully. Astrid was at a table with her two children, Ottar and Inga, along with Runa and some of the other elders. I caught her eye and she nodded. It was time.

I grabbed Agnarr's hand as I stood. Astrid stood as well. As we walked to the center of the gathering a hush fell over the crowd, all eyes on us. Astrid stood in front with Agnarr and me slightly behind her. I leaned in closer to Agnarr, nervous, as Astrid addressed the crowd.

"Welcome! Welcome all to Fýrifírar! We are so pleased to finally meet and welcome our new members!" Astrid beamed at the crowd, "This is a sign of a new chapter for the Fýrifírar Tribe. Our new members will provide new insight and visions for the future. Our new jarl and jarlin will provide the balanced leadership we need in this time of change—"

"Já, and what if we don't want this *change*?" A voice growled from the back of the crowd.

I'd been watching Astrid and hadn't noticed Magna and the dozen other orkin who hadn't been at the celebration arrive. They were all male, mostly elder, but with a few that appeared to be around my age. Magna stood, arms folded across his chest. I blanched. I'd tried very hard not to let the other women be exposed to this ugly side of the elder members of the tribe. I watched as they shifted position in the crowd, gathering near Billie, who was the de facto leader in my absence. She looked confused, but not scared.

My eyes whipped back to Astrid. She didn't skip a beat.

"Those that are unwilling to accept change will not be welcome in the tribe. Either accept the new members and the new leadership or leave," she said coolly.

"This is our tribe too. We've been here just as long as you. I remember when you were nothing but a young gardener before you were claimed by Ulf," Magna sneered.

"You display a fundamental misunderstanding of how the

Elska bond works. Ulf did not choose me. Our marks appeared and we chose each other. A female is not something to be claimed," Astrid responded with an icy tone.

My eyes whipped back and forth between Astrid and Magna. I felt like I was on the Jerry Springer show or an overly dramatic episode of the Kardashians. Magna's eyes narrowed and he turned to assess me and Agnarr as we stood to the right of Astrid, ready to be introduced.

"So you're saying the Elska bond felt this weak, pale thing worthy of our new jarl?" He waved vaguely at me.

At this, Agnarr left my side and swiftly started moving through the crowd toward Magna. I brought my fist to my mouth, biting on my knuckle, afraid of what Agnarrr would do to Magna. But Skaard got there first. He approached his father with no hesitation, hauled back, and punched him squarely in the face. My jaw dropped to the ground. If it weren't so serious, I would want popcorn. Magna stumbled back, caught by who I assumed was his youngest son, Ozur. He was shooting daggers at Skaard, who had since been joined by Iric, Agnarr, and several of the guards, including Vott. Magna's nose was bleeding rapidly, but he shook off those who attempted to help him.

He looked at Skaard with disgust, "So, this is the side you choose?"

"This is the side of the future, I have no desire to live in the past."

"And you're willing to *mate* with one of these humans?" he asked in disbelief.

"I doubt any of them will have me now that they've seen who my father is, but yes. I am."

"Fine. Fine," Magna spit, "We're leaving. I hope you all have puny offspring that are killed off in the next tribal skirmish."

With that, he and his small group of followers turned and

left the celebration, with only Ozur giving Skaard the briefest of looks before following his father. There was a moment of stunned silence before the entire tribe erupted.

"Silence," Astrid commanded.

It was at that moment I fully understood how she'd led Fýrifírar for so long without Ulf. She may be petite, for an orc, but at the sound of her voice, the entire tribe stepped in line.

"Now that we have unfortunately witnessed how orkin who disagree with our path forward will be dispensed with, it is time to introduce our new jarl and jarlin. " She gestured toward Agnarr, who'd rejoined my side and me to move forward.

I did, hesitantly at first, but with Agnarr's reassuring grip at my waist, I tried to put on my best 'I can handle anything' smile. If teaching through all of the crises of the 2000s taught me anything, it was to just keep smiling. It's fine. It's all fine. I was reminded of my first year of teaching where I thought I could teach September 11th. I cried the entire day and scared all of my students. Clearly an excellent teacher. Every year after that I took September 11th off and went to Disneyland. This was how I felt at that moment, I had to either keep up the facade or I'd crumble. Agnarr and I stepped forward.

"Jarl Agnarr and Jarlin Piper will be the new leaders of our tribe in two cycles of the moon. They will be guided by me in all ways as we forge a path forward. With our new tribe members and the course we are going to take, having a human jarlin and an orkin jarl could not be more suitable for Fýrifírar," Astrid announced to thunderous applause from human and orkin alike.

I stood there, bemused, trying to gain footing after all that happened, when Agnarr grabbed me by the waist and turned me to him. He kissed me thoroughly in front of the entire tribe, hands at my waist, melding us together. The cheers grew even louder as Astrid stepped back and the entire tribe rejoiced in our leadership and our pairing. There was a small part of my brain that was horrified at the attention, but the rest of me rejoiced at the acceptance and I slid my fingers up into Agnarr's braid, pulling him to me, kissing him completely. When we parted I looked for any hesitation in Agnarr's eyes but found only smug triumph. I grinned before turning to the crowd to find hands clapping and lewd hollering.

CHAPTER 16

AGNARR

*A*strid and I had planned for Piper and me to address the crowd, but cutting the speeches short seemed for the best after what happened with Magna. Piper had plastered on her fake smile, and I had no idea where her head was. It took all of my control not to race after Magna and beat him to a pulp. The insults he threw directly at Piper called for nothing less than bloodshed. I was surprised, but not upset, that Skaard got to him before I did. Though I wanted to get my hands on Magna, throttling an ousted elder before the entire tribe wouldn't be a good look for the new jarl. Skaard's willingness to tear apart his family for the sake of the tribe spoke volumes. We were lucky to have him on the council.

While Piper snaked through the crowd to check in with the human women, I went to Astrid. She'd sat at one of the tables with some of the other elders and was helping herself to a plate of food. Though she wouldn't crack in front of the tribe, I could tell she was tired. She was tired of all of this. I sat down beside her, nodding to the other elders in greeting.

"Well, that didn't go exactly as planned," I said lightly, bringing my drink to my lips.

"Hardly."

"Are you worried?"

"About Magna? No. He and the rest of his group will be lucky if they make it to the next tribe. They're all old and not suited for long travel. If they get attacked by anything or come across unfriendly orkin, they are done for."

"What about the tribe?"

"Look around you. Do you see a reason to worry?"

At this, I took a few minutes to assess the rest of the tribe. I immediately zeroed in on Piper. She was with several of the other women. I recognized Billie from her mane of wild curly hair, which I'd never seen in orkin. She was going to be a hot commodity based on her hair alone. The rest of the women I was still getting to know. They were sitting with Osif, of all people. They looked engaged in a very in-depth conversation, but no one appeared uncomfortable. I had a sneaking suspicion that Piper had secret plans with Osif, but whenever I asked him about it he told me all their conversations had been about the housing for the women. I eyed them shrewdly for a second longer, wondering if Osif was simply an excellent secret keeper, before looking around at the rest of the crowd.

Most of the human women were in twos or threes but talking animatedly to orkin, male and female alike. No one appeared uncomfortable. I was surprised to see Skaard seated with just one human woman, talking quietly. If I remembered correctly, her name was Zoey. She was one of the humans with a traumatic past. I assessed them carefully, but both seemed at ease. They weren't sitting close, but they were engaged in conversation. Looking at the tribe, the damper on the mood that Magna and his followers had cast upon our celebration had dissipated.

"See?" Astrid said, "It is all going to be fine."

I made a noncommittal noise before taking another sip of my drink. Even if everyone seemed happy now, I expected turbulence as the human women assimilated and the tribe tested Piper and me as their new leaders. Astrid had been the Jardin for almost two tiårs on her own and longer than that with Ulf. This would be a massive shift for Fýrifírar. I worried for Piper. Even with all the groundwork we were laying, I worried about what it would cost her to carry all the fears and concerns of the human women. I knew she didn't need to—she knew she didn't need to—but she was.

I let my eyes drift to her again. She was still in animated conversation with Osif, Billie, and several of the women. I lingered on Billie. Piper seemed to spend the most time with Billie of all the women. She mentioned having similar upbringings. I wondered if I should speak to Billie about alleviating some of Piper's concerns—or at least helping me convince Piper that she didn't have to mother all of them. As if aware of my eyes on her, Billie looked up and flashed me a smile. I smiled easily back, raising my cup to her. My plan started to solidify. I'd talk to Billie about how to help Piper be the best leader she could be. I shifted to find Piper's gaze on me. She looked me up and down, making her thoughts very plain. My nostrils flared, and I could almost sense the shift in her smell, even from the distance. I wondered if it was too early for us to sneak away. I looked out to find Astrid smiling at me smugly.

"Mating frenzy still in effect?" She grinned.

"Does it ever go away?" I asked.

"It will, in time, it will. But do you want it to right now?"

My cheeks darkened, and I took a sip of my drink to avoid having to answer.

"Go," she said, "no one will think anything of it."

I didn't need to be told twice. I left my chair and my drink without a look back. Piper was focused on her conversation with Osif and the other women. I took the opportunity to sneak up behind her.

I leaned down and growled into her ear, "I think it is past your bedtime."

Pip gave a startled yelp and looked up at me.

She playfully swatted my arm, "Don't scare me like that!" she said, cheeks flushed.

"But then I wouldn't get to see the lovely shade of pink your cheeks go," I retorted.

Her cheeks went a darker shade of pink, and I couldn't help myself. She looked so delightful. I leaned over and scooped her out of her chair then turned and walked away from the group with her in my arms.

"Hey! I can walk!" Pip shrieked.

"I feel like we've had this conversation several times now. I like to carry you."

"But—"

"I am sure Billie will manage just fine. You should lean on her for support. She seems more than capable."

"She *is* capable. And charming. She's the extrovert I need when it gets too crowded, and my brain starts to short circuit."

"Would you want to give her an official title?"

"I hadn't really thought about it."

"What if we made her the elder that represented the human women?" Pip looked pensive.

"Isn't that kind of my job?" she asked.

"No, your job is to lead the tribe alongside me. You don't have to be responsible for the humans. I know you will always *feel* responsible, but you could share some of that with Billie," I explained gently.

She stroked my tunic's soft fabric, tracing the embroidery's outline with a finger before looking up at me.

"Is it okay if I think about it?"

"Of course it is," I said, brushing my lips to her temple.

"Okay, now that that's settled, can we discuss how you dragged me away from the celebration like you owned me?" she said tartly.

"I could smell you. You have needs."

Pip let out a garbled string of what seemed to be embarrassment and indignation but no coherent words, all while covering her bright red face.

"Would you like to try that again?" I grinned down at her.

She huffed out a breath and looked up at me, clearly irritated.

"First, it is ridiculously unfair that you can smell whenever I am..." she trailed off, clearly too embarrassed to even say it out loud.

"In need of your orc?" I suggested.

She rolled her eyes, "Fine, let's call it that. Second, you can't just whisk me away every time you... every time you... smell me," she finished lamely.

"And why not?" I asked, looking at her hungrily.

"What if we're in the middle of an important meeting?" she asked, exasperated.

"What has happened in the meeting to make you aroused?" I teased.

"Have you seen you?! You hulking, gorgeous lumbersnack? And now that I know what you're capable of, I'm a goner."

"Oh, and what am I capable of, sweet Pip?" I whispered, still striding towards my room.

Pip pursed her lips, clearly irritated that I was making her spell it out.

"Before you, I was lucky if I orgasmed at all with a partner. My enjoyment was never part of the equation. Now..." She trailed off, looking away from me, clearly uncomfortable with this conversation.

Pip had a lot of hangups when it came to sex, even though she attempted to fight through them with me. It was time for me to stop teasing her. She'd been a willing and enthusiastic partner in bed with me, but she carried a lot of shame from her experiences.

I took her chin in my hand, pulling her to face me, "Pip, if I scent you in the middle of a meeting, or a celebration, or the middle of the evening meal, I will absolutely throw you over my shoulder and carry you back to my room or our home. None of the orkin will think twice about it. They know how strong the mating bond is. There is no meeting that could stop me from making sure your needs are met."

It's almost as if she's tapped out of embarrassment and couldn't muster another protest, "Well then. If that's the norm, I guess that is something I could get used to... maybe." She still looked like she found the whole thing mortifying, so I dropped it.

When we reached my room, I opened the door wordlessly with Pip still in my arms. My room was dark and chilly. I gently set Pip on my bed and got to work building a fire. Before long, the flames danced merrily, and I could turn my attention to Piper.

As the fire warmed the room, I pulled off my tunic. I watched as she observed me, clearly appreciating all the muscle that was on display. Pip chewed at her lower lip as I approached her.

"Ready to join me?" she said, voice breathy.

I was ready to stumble into bed with my Pip, but I was still wearing too much clothing. I shucked my boots quickly before unlacing my leather pants, all while Pip watched, the appreciation evident in her eyes.

"Enjoying the show?" I questioned, unlacing my pants.

"Absolutely," she responded, grinning at me.

Pip pulled the covers over her shoulders, hiding her from my gaze. All I could see was her face, smiling at me as I undressed. Finally naked, she scooted over in bed to allow me to join her. I lifted the covers and slipped in, pulling her toward me immediately. The delighted grumble I made when I realized she was completely naked under the covers earned me a soft giggle.

"Is this what you were hoping for?" she asked.

"This is exactly what I was hoping for," I murmured, kissing down her neck.

I settled my body over hers, kissing and stroking her everywhere. I lived for her quiet sounds of pleasure as I stroked down her sides and nipped at her breasts.

"What did you have in mind for tonight, my dear Pip?" I murmured, not taking my eyes off her chest while licking her nipples into stiff peaks.

"I need you to fuck me. Nothing—nothing compares to how well you fill me with your cock," she said, breathing hitched.

"Can I have a taste first?" I asked, skimming my lips down from her breasts, kissing my way down her torso.

Pip squirmed beneath me, threading her fingers through my hair, "Yes, yes, please."

I growled in approval. We'd come so far. I was reminded of our first time together, where Pip had snapped her thighs shut at the idea of my mouth on her. Now she was bare before me, legs spread wide, ready and willing. I continued my kisses down her torso, kissing down her hip bone before continuing lower. The smell of her arousal was heady as I reached her cunt. She was so pink and perfect. I slid my arms under her thighs, pulling her wider as I dipped down, licking her hot slit. Pip's grasp of my hair tightened as I licked her up and down before circling my tongue around her sensitive clit.

"More, more. I need your fingers," she moaned.

I continued to lap at her clit while thrusting a finger into her. I could feel her clamp down on me, desperate for the intrusion, bucking against my face. This was the Pip I loved, untethered and unworried, wholly focused on her pleasure. I continued to thrust in and out of her, adding a second finger, all while still suckling at her clit. I loved every gasp and cry she gave me, every jolt of pleasure I felt strum through her body. I felt her gasp rip through. Her thighs locked around my head the same way her cunt locked down on my fingers, and I was flooded with her release. I continued to lick her, slowing my pace to let her come down from her climax. Pip's grip loosened, and her legs fell open as she went limp. I kissed my way back up her body before leaning over her and looking at her beautifully flushed face.

Piper

Agnarr smirked above me, supporting himself on his elbows, knowing he'd just given me a mind-blowing orgasm in record time. Before Agnarr, I'd never been multi-orgasmic. Heck, I'd never been orgasmic. An orgasm was an unexpected delight—not a regularity. Because of my upbringing, I was well into my twenties before I understood what would get me off. Sharing that with a partner was a massive hurdle for me. Although Agnarr and I had hiccups, he'd brought me more satisfaction and understanding than any prior partner. I tried my best to let go of my former hangups, but I would be lying if I said they weren't there in the back of my mind. Maybe Agnarr wouldn't want me because of my insecurities. Perhaps he wanted a mate without baggage or trauma.

While Agnarr continued to lick me up and down as I

came down from my climax, and I wanted nothing more than to return the favor. Now that he was grinning over me, I quickly pushed him away, rolling us so he was on his back. Agnarr grunted at the shove, then looked up at me in surprise.

"What's this, Pip?" he asked, voice low, "I thought you wanted my cock."

"Oh, I do want your cock. Just in more ways than one," I teased, leaning to kiss down his neck.

Agnarr shuddered underneath me as I licked my way down his hardened body. I paused to trace my tongue over each nipple, then down to his navel. I wanted to savor him the way he had cherished me. I traced my tongue down his stomach before pulling back to admire his cock. Thick and textured, the tip pooled with pre-cum. My core felt empty and clenched, wanting desperately to be filled again, but I wanted to taste him first. I would never tire of watching him come undone with my mouth on him.

I placed my hands on either side of his hips and dragged my tongue slowly along the underside of his cock, pausing to tease the sensitive skin. Agnarr groaned beneath me, his cock kicking forward at attention. I looked at him to see his gaze hooded with lust. I took the head of his cock and slid him down as far as I could go, feeling him bump against the back of my throat. This still left a good portion of his cock unattended, so I added my hands into my ministrations. I stroked the base of him up and down while I sucked down the rest of his length in rhythm. Agnarr's hands clutched the bedding with white-knuckled determination, and I wanted him untethered. I slid my mouth off him with a pop, still stroking him up and down with my hand.

"You can set the pace, you know. I want your hands in my hair, guiding me, showing me what you like," I had said this to him before, but it was as if he was hesitant to show me exactly what would see him undone. He didn't want to push me into anything.

Agnarr slid his fingers into my hair at the base of my head, wrapping his fingers into my hair and guided me back to his cock. I opened eagerly, wanting him to be in control, sucking down his cock while gripping him firmly. He grasped my head with both hands, guiding my pace as I sucked him. He set a punishing pace, bumping against the back of my throat with every thrust. I loved every second of it. I'd longed for a partner who was open about his wants and needs instead of hiding them and forcing me to attempt to figure them out.

I sucked Agnarr up and down while still working him with my hands. His cock grew harder at my attention, and I continued to suck him withenthusiasm until he suddenly pulled me off of him by the roots of my hair. I looked up at him, eyes hooded and mind addled with lust as he held me roughly by my scalp.

"I want to cum inside you, my mate, and that won't happen if you continue as you have been," he rasped.

I could barely nod, with how he held my head, but I jerked my chin down to show my assent. He grabbed me by the hips and positioned me on my knees and elbows in front of him, spread wide. Agnarr thrust a thick finger into me, pushing in and out quickly, with how wet I was. I moaned and pushed myself back, silently asking for more. He added another finger, stretching me to accommodate him, thrusting in and out with his fingers as I panted into the pillow.

"Agnarr," I groaned, "It's not enough," as he continued to pump in and out of me.

"Are you ready for—what was it you called it—my monster cock?" he teased.

"So ready," I breathed.

Agnarr slid his fingers out of me, and I groaned at the emptiness I felt. But he quickly replaced his fingers with the head of his cock, pressed against my entrance. I gasped at the pressure. I would never cease to be surprised at the girth of Agnarr, even as he slowly pushed into me. I could feel every ridge and braid along his textured member, clamping down on him as he slid into me. I groaned as he thrust to the hilt, our thighs touching as he bottomed out inside me. This was the fullness I wanted. The stretch of him was indescribable. Every ridge and braid dragged along my already sensitive walls. I panted as he thrust in and out of me, slow and heavy, allowing me to adjust to his size. Agnarr only gave me a few moments to change before he was snapping into me, hips pressing against my ass, clearly on the brink.

With all the previous attention, I was ready to fall over the edge with him; I just needed a *little* more. I grabbed one of his hands from my hip and pulled it down to my pussy. Agnarr took no time at all to understand what I was asking. His fingers skated down my folds, parting me to stroke a calloused thumb against my clit. Between that and his steady thrusts, I was done for. I locked down underneath him, my muscles tensing, coming with a strangled scream of his name as he hammered into me.

With just one—two more thrusts, I felt the kick of his cock and the warm release of him flooding me. He spasmed over me, planting his hands on either side of my head to keep from crushing me beneath him. Sliding his arms underneath mine, he pulled me to him, holding me closely as we returned to reality. I was a boneless mess of bliss as he nuzzled my temple and kissed down my neck, still locked inside me.

"Pip," he murmured against my temple.

"I'm here. I'm always here."

CHAPTER 17

*P*iper
 I awoke to find Agnarr gripping me tightly, a leg thrown over my hip, and my breast cupped in his hand. Even in his sleep, Agnarr was ready to devour me whole. I took a few steadying breaths before scooting out of his embrace. Not only was I overly warm from his fiery hold, but I needed to pee desperately. I carefully extricated myself as he continued to sleep, rushing to the toilet.

After relieving myself and thoroughly cleaning any mess from the prior evening, I looked in the mirror. My lips were pink and swollen from Agnarr's kisses. Other than that, I looked calm, collected. A way I hadn't felt in months, maybe years. I rinsed my face and patted myself dry before rejoining Agnarr in his bed. I longed for a day when it would be *our* bed, but that would come soon enough. The sun was barely a faint sliver on the horizon. Knowing that Agnarr would sleep for at least another hour, I pressed myself into him, relishing in the comfort and warmth. Agnarr shifted without waking, wrapping me back in his arms.

I started a mental to-do list for the day. I wasn't an early riser usually, but we both had a lot to accomplish. In less than two months, we would take over from Astrid. I needed to check in with Osif on the quarters for the human women. We had agreed on a dorm-like situation, with each woman getting their own room and toilet, but sharing a shower—or sauna, as they called it here. It was coming along nicely, and Osif was confident it would be finished within the next three weeks. He and Billie got along well. I wondered if this was something I could hand off to her, thinking of the conversation I'd had with Agnarr the previous evening.

Billie was more than capable of leading the human women. She was the most outgoing of the group and displayed leadership capabilities. Back on Earth, she had worked her way up from host to managing bartender at her restaurant. She was lively and confident and made friends quickly. I could see the appeal of making her the elder for the females. If I handed off the construction project of the rooms for the humans, I could focus more on the tribe as a whole— and my secret project for our new home. I was still hesitant. It felt almost lazy to let Billie take on representing the human women. I pushed the thought out of my mind. That was my teacher's brain talking—the one where I was expected to do everything and be everything for everyone. If Agnarr wanted to have Billie to support me, I would accept it.

As soon as the thought formed, I could feel my shoulders unclench and my stomach settle. My body was telling me it was the right decision. I'd talk to her about it today. Knowing Billie, she'd be willing and eager to embrace the new role. I snuggled into Agnarr, trying to decide if I could sleep a bit more or if my brain was done letting me rest. I felt his heart beat slowly against me and his steady breath. His warm arms wrapped around me, unconsciously providing me warmth and comfort. It wasn't long before sleep found me.

I awoke to a soft rap at the door about an hour later,

judging by how the light flowed into the room. I was still wrapped in Agnarr's arms but slipped out of his embrace without waking him. I padded softly toward the door. I opened it just wide enough to retrieve the tray that was left, not wanting the morning light to wake Agnarr. I took the tray to the low table before the fire and took inventory of what we'd been provided. There were pastries upon pastries piled high. There was also a large serving of gautr with all of the accompanying toppings. The tray was rounded out with a kettle of hot water and several different teas. Ignoring the teas on the tray, I pulled open one of the dresser's drawers and extracted some of the baldrian root. I set it away to steep in one of the earthenware cups as I helped myself to a generous serving of gautr and a few pastries.

I sat quietly, munching away at the delicious breakfast—once again in awe of communal meal practices. Back on Earth, my breakfast was a venti iced latte with sugar-free vanilla and 2% milk. And a string cheese. Though I definitely missed the coffee, this breakfast was much better. At the very least, it wouldn't lead me to a panic attack during the first block of classes. I allowed myself to drift back to the classroom, thinking about bathroom passes and late homework. I was so lost in thought that I didn't hear Agnarr approach me from behind. I gasped at the warm breath against my ear.

"Having breakfast without me?" Agnarr grumbled softly.

"I wanted to let you sleep," I responded, leaning into him, savoring his warmth against my neck.

"Well, I am awake now and more than ready for breakfast," he murmured into my neck before joining me in front of the fire.

Agnarr took several pastries and twice as much gautr as I could consume, covering it liberally with syrup and dried fruits, before sitting next to me in front of the fire. I made a garbled noise in my throat, watching Agnarr sit and prepare to eat, fully nude. Eating breakfast with a naked Agnarr was a bit more than I was prepared for.

Hearing my unintelligible shock, Agnarr looked up at me, brow raised, "Is this too much for you?"

"Well—you're naked. How can I focus on breakfast with my naked mate sitting beside me?" I said, my voice sounding somewhat hysterical.

Agnarr huffed a laugh before setting his meal aside. He headed to the dresser, pulled out a fresh pair of leggings, and pulled them on before returning to our breakfast. While I appreciated him fully on display, I would never be able to finish my breakfast if he sat there eating, covered by nothing but his tray of food. I was grateful for the leggings. We continued to eat in companionable silence as Agnarr reached out and gently stroked his fingers up and down my thigh.

"What did you have planned for today?" he asked.

"I was hoping to speak with Billie today about taking on more of a leadership role for the human women. I'm going to ask her to join the elders," I said.

Agnarr nodded thoughtfully. "So you've accepted my proposal? Billie has many qualities that would suit the position."

"My thoughts exactly. I'd also like her to oversee the new living quarters project with Osif so that I could focus more on the tribe as a whole."

"You have my full support, Piper. I'm pleased to see you empowering others to use their talents," Agnarr replied.

We discussed our plans for the day and how to include more voices in shaping the tribe, with the addition of the human women. Agnarr would meet with Astrid while I met with Billie and Osif. I was still finding my way but was grateful to have a partner committed to building a community based on our shared values. Though we came from different worlds, Agnarr and I shared the same ideals. We wanted everyone to feel seen and heard, regardless of background.

After finishing breakfast Agnarr returned to the dresser, pulling on a tunic to match his leggings, before approaching me expectantly.

Right. This was something I was still getting used to. Agnarr needed me to braid his hair. Over the last few weeks, Saela and Tora taught me several intricate braids. Agnarr was to be jarl, he needed his plaits to be perfect. I paused to gather some of the beads I had collected from some of the other mated females, incorporating them into the design of his braids as I continued to maneuver his beautiful locks. He leaned into me, exhaling softly at the attention I was giving him. I finished what I would call a double Dutch braid that wove together at the base of his skull and tied it with a piece of leather.

I stood back and surveyed my work.

"It looks respectable," I murmured. "With time and practice, I'll do better."

"I am sure it looks amazing," Agnarr said, pulling me to him.

He was still seated, giving him full access to me while I stood. His fingers roved along the swell of my ass before grabbing it firmly. He pulled me to him, smelling me as I pressed into him.

"You're in want of your orc," he said knowingly.

I cursed his ability to scent when I was aroused before finding my voice. "Perhaps I am, but you and I both have responsibilities to attend to," regretfully pulling myself from his embrace.

Agnarr looked at me, face full of want, but let me slide out of his grip.

I dressed myself until we were both ready to meet the tribe.

We headed to the door of his room before parting ways. He pulled me close and brushed a kiss to my temple before heading off toward the center of the village. I waited for a beat, glowing from the embrace, before heading toward the smithy. I arrived to find Billie and Osif already engaged in animated conversation. Osif had initially hesitated about Billie, having never experienced a female so outgoing and forthright, but they'd come to solid common ground. It was clear, as I approached that I was no longer needed in these conversations.

"Hi, y'all!" I said, grinning with authentic enthusiasm.

"Piper!" Billie crushed me into an embrace.

I was learning to accept physical attention in many different ways—hugs being one of them. Instead of going stiff, as I would have in the past, I welcomed Billie's embrace, pulling her into me. I realized with Billie that I didn't hate hugs. I hated hesitant hugs. So many people gave hugs that they weren't really interested in providing. Like, if you don't want to hug me, don't bother.

Billie's hugs were never hesitant, and I accepted her with open arms. She pulled back from me, eyes shining."Do you want to see what we are working on?"

"Of course!"

I sat down at the workbench that Osif and Billie were working at, examining the plans and proposals laid across the table.

"Any hiccups?" I asked.

Osif and Billie exchanged glances for a moment before Billie responded.

"Well, there is going to be extra work involved in adding a sauna and bathing situation for the humans, but once I explained to Osif human modesty, he was willing to take on the extra work."

"Já, I did not know communal bathing was outside the

norm for the humans. I am making adjustments to allow for that," Osif explained.

"As always, Osif, I appreciate your willingness to adjust to human customs," I smiled warmly at Osif, grateful for his adaptability and kindness toward us newcomers. Though I had grown more comfortable with the norms of Fýrifírar culture, I knew many of the human women would appreciate some concessions.

We continued examining the plans and discussing layouts and materials. I was impressed by how thoughtfully Billie and Osif had approached designing accommodations to meet the needs of the different groups.

"I think this all looks wonderful," I said finally. "You've both put so much care into ensuring everyone feels comfortable and respected here. I'm thrilled with the progress."

Billie beamed at the praise. "Well, thanks, Piper. We're excited, too. It'll be nice having our own space while still being close to the heart of things."

"Absolutely," I agreed. I took a breath before continuing. "Speaking of being at the heart of things, I wanted to talk to you about taking on more of a leadership role among the group."

Billie's eyes widened in surprise. "Me? Really?"

I nodded, "You're a natural leader, Billie. The women respect you and feel comfortable coming to you with questions or concerns. And I know from our time on Earth how skilled you are at managing people and projects."

Billie looked thoughtful as she considered my words. "I think it would change things a bit if I had some sort of official title, but you know I'd do anything for you. I'll step up if you and the other elders think it would help."

"It would help tremendously," I assured her. I glanced at Osif. "What do you think about Billie joining the council to represent the human women?"

Osif inclined his head respectfully. "I believe she will serve well in such a role."

I smiled, laying a hand on Billie's shoulder. "Then it's settled. We'll announce the next council meeting. Thank you, Billie. I'm grateful to have you supporting me and our people."

Billie pulled me into another quick, fierce hug. "Happy to do it," she said. As we pulled apart, her expression grew more serious. "And just know I've got your back, Piper. However I can help lift some of the burden from you, I'm here."

Her heartfelt words nearly brought me to tears. But I just nodded, hoping she could read the depths of my gratitude. With Billie joining leadership, the future of Fýrifírar felt brighter than ever. Billie and I left Osif, and I wanted time with just her.

As we left Osif's cabin, Billie and I walked arm in arm.

"What are you thinking?" I asked eventually.

"I think you have been given an enormous burden of being the new jarlin and a human. I know that there are orkin who have left the tribe over the addition of the human women, and I know that there are orkin who are undecided. It is a steep hill to climb," she said plainly.

"Mmm," I assented.

"Given all that has taken place, I would be happy to join the council of elders as the representative for the humans. You have enough on your plate already" she paused, shifting the topic. "How are things with you outside the jarl jarlin thing?"

I blushed. I knew what she was asking about. Billie was the only person I'd been fully transparent with about being mated to an orc. I'd given all the women a basic anatomy lesson and assured them that everything fit just fine, but it was harder for me to go into details while being seen as their leader. Billie knew about the accidental hickeys, the hair-pulling, and the mind-blowing orgasms. We'd both been raised in the church and had left it as adults, so I felt a sense of kinship with her. *No bonding like trauma bonding.*

"Honestly, still amazing. If you'd told me I would be having sex multiple times a day six months ago, I would have looked at you like you were insane, but that seems to be the norm for mates, according to Saela and Tora," I said, grinning, but looking down at the path.

Billie looked wistful. I knew she was more than ready to have a mate, she'd confided in me that she'd been very unhappily single on Earth. She'd had several casual relationships, but nothing that stuck. I truly hoped she found someone here.

"We're still learning to communicate, though," I offered. "I'm not used to having a partner who is even interested in my needs, let alone asking me to voice them. It's awkward at first," I said truthfully.

"I get that. When I first really started dating and figured out what I liked, it took me a long time to verbalize it, let alone expect it. Does Agnarr—" she paused, fishing for the right words, "Does he respond to your requests?"

I laughed quietly, "I think Agnarr would do anything I asked. It is just me getting used to asking. He likes things just a bit on the rougher side, and I am definitely down with being thrown about a little."

"Any regrets? About being fate-bonded to an orc rather than married to a human man?" she asked mischievously.

I laughed, "The last dude I was with wouldn't even go down on me unless I was waxed bare and straight out of the shower. Even then, he treated it as a chore. Who's going to get off that way?"

"No one," she deadpanned.

We both broke out in a fit of giggles.

"But seriously, you're happy? Are you ready to take this on? As one of the few people you've let in, I am asking."

"I am deliriously happy with Agnarr. Heck, if he weren't working on the future of the tribe with Astrid right now, I'd have him bending me over the edge of his bed," I said, smirking as the image came to mind.

"I know you have some surprises in store for him at your new home," Billie dropped casually.

I gasped in mock indignation, "Osif's been letting you in on my secrets!"

"Of course he has," she chuckled, "he knows I won't tell a soul."

"And that is why I am trusting the two of you to take on the housing for the women," I said emphatically.

"Well, there is one more thing I would like to take on, if you are interested," Billie said, looking almost nervous.

"Oooh, what secrets do you have up your sleeve?" I asked, teasingly.

"Well if it was *me* and I was the first human female to accept a mate bond *and* about to become jarlin, I'd want a wedding," she said.

I stopped in my tracks, arm still looped in Billie's.

"Like a wedding, wedding?" I asked.

"Why not? Are you any less than married? If anything, you're more than married."

"Well—yes, but they don't seem to do weddings here."

"Didn't you do a whole bunch of weird ceremonial shit in a pool in a *cave*?" she pressed.

"Yes, yes, I did do that."

"So, would a standard human wedding be so much to ask?" she quipped.

I laughed ruefully.

"If you are worried about teaching a bunch of orkin to do the YMCA, you can skip that part," she teased.

I snorted at the idea of trying to do the YMCA with the members of Fýrifírar. I wouldn't even do that if I were marrying a human. But I did let my mind drift. I'd imagined getting married one day. White gown, veil, the whole shebang. Mating with Agnarr had changed everything. Yet the idea of him and I exchanging vows in front of Fýrifírar was definitely something that made my heart rate go up. Astrid would officiate, of course. I would have all the women involved as bridesmaids, or greeters. Little Odin could be the ring bearer. I smiled, thinking how happy he would be to be charged with such an important role.

Billie brought me back from my thoughts by nudging me in the ribs, "See? You want a wedding," she said. "And so will many of the other women, if they take on mates. I think you should set the tone."

I sighed, "Yes, a traditional wedding would be something I would be interested in. But with all Agnarr has on his plate already, it is too much to ask."

"Why don't you let me handle that?" she asked, grinning at me.

"Handle what?"

"Let me walk Agnarr through an American wedding and see what he thinks," she said, grinning at me.

Oh boy, I wasn't sure if I was ready to hand *this* off to Billie. What if Agnarr was completely overwhelmed by the idea? What if it was too weird for him?

Seeing the hesitancy in my eyes, Billie squeezed my hand.

"Will you let me talk to Agnarr?" she asked.

"About the wedding?"

"Of course! If it is what human women expect, I should be the one to bring it to the table. They shouldn't give up a tradition they love just because they are here," she said sincerely.

I rolled it around in my head for a moment. I trusted

Billie completely, and she was right. Many of the human women would want weddings. I would be the one to set the standard.

"Alright. You can talk to Agnarr about it. But I have one request," I said.

"And that is?"

"I absolutely do not want to do a garter toss. I think it's gross and weird. Also, I am walking myself down the aisle. No one is giving me away. I am my own person, " I explained.

"Noted," she said with a laugh.

We continued down the path toward the longhouse for the midday meal. I felt myself unclench, at ease in Billie's presence. She was a good choice as a second-in-command, in all ways.

CHAPTER 18

AGNARR

The meeting with Astrid went well. She was pleased with the progress and was no longer concerned about the orkin acceptance of the humans now that Magna and his followers had left. All signs pointed toward a smooth transition. I relayed the decision to add Billie to the council of elders, and she was happy with the choice. Astrid agreed that Piper having another human to lean on for support would allow her to lead the tribe more effectively. I left Astrid's home and headed to the longhouse.

I pushed open the double doors of the longhouse to find it full of orkin and humans alike enjoying the midday meal. I surveyed the room for my Pip, but Billie's wild mane of hair caught my eyes first. She and Piper were sitting at a table full of humans, and I hesitated momentarily. I wasn't sure if I should interrupt, but the desire to be near my mate was so strong that I grabbed some food and headed toward them. Pip looked up as I approached.

"Hello, my lovely lumbersnack," she said, grinning. "We were just talking about you."

At this, the table erupted in a fit of giggles.

"All good things, I hope?" I said as I took a seat.

"Only the best things," Piper said mischievously.

Ah, it was one of those conversations. From what Piper had told me, many of the human women were desperate for more details about not only finding an Elksa mate but bedding an orc in general. At this point, she was the only human that had the details. I felt my face grow warm, knowing they were likely talking about my anatomy and our sex life, but I tried tamping it down to the best of my ability. This was all unknown to them. They had the right to ask questions. I dug into my plate of food, trying to ignore the obvious stares I was receiving.

Billie spoke first, of course, "Can you tell me, Agnarr, do all males have braided and ridged cocks, or is that just a you thing?"

I choked on the meat pie I was eating. I looked at Piper to see if she actually expected me to answer the question, and while her cheeks were flaming red, she just nodded in encouragement.

I managed to swallow my mouth full of food and took a swig of drink, trying to steady myself.

"While I can't say I have seen all of my tribe members' cocks up close, all orkin penises have a braided texture of some pattern. The pattern is different based on the male," I mumbled, looking anywhere but Billie's eyes.

"Hmmm," Billie thrummed her fingers against her lips, "And is it true that orkin don't kiss?"

Registering how hot my face felt, I knew I must be an intense shade of green.

"Well, I can't say that I have asked any of the other males, but it definitely wasn't something I had experienced before.

It was a, um, a welcome surprise," I finished, somewhat lamely.

"And is it true that Pip was your first blow job?" Billie continued, completely unabashed.

At this, Piper put her face in her hands, the redness of her skin matching the green of mine. "Billie," she groaned.

"What? We need to know what we're getting into," Billie said, completely unapologetic.

"Yes, yes that is true," I said, not giving anything further.

"But it's normal for males to go down on their females?" another woman, whose name I didn't know, piped up.

"Well. Given the nature of our cocks, it is necessary to ensure our females are wet and ready to take— er...to... proceed. That and most males I know find pleasuring their partner in that way quite enjoyable," I explained, my voice coming out raspy.

"Enough, enough!" Piper said. She was a lovely shade of pink but smiling, "You've interrogated Agnarr enough for today. I promise I will make him available for more questions, but for now, can we let him eat?"

All of the women looked crestfallen that Pip had stopped the line of questioning, but they gave me a reprieve. I reached under the table and rested my hand on Pip's thigh. She gripped my hand and grinned before returning to her food.

"Okay, so before we were so rudely interrupted, I believe we were discussing the progress on your new living quarters?" she said, giving Billie a rueful look.

Billie smirked, utterly unfazed by the reprimand from Pip, and returned to addressing the women as a whole.

"Osif believes that we will be ready to move in the week after next if all goes according to plan."

"That sounds lovely," a petite woman, who I believed was called Joanna, said.

The women all nodded in assent.

"Are you all—" I halted, looking for words, "Are you comfortable enough while you wait for your accommodations to be built?"

"We feel bad for displacing some of the orkin, but we're more than comfortable," a curvy woman, Ginny I think, responded.

"Those displaced don't mind. They have already readily accepted you into the tribe, but I am sure they will be happy things are moving along smoothly," I replied.

"Speaking of, we need to get back to Osif's team," Pip said, standing and looking at Billie.

"Go on without me. I wanted to talk with Agnarr a bit more," Billie responded.

Pip's brows went dangerously high, "Billie..." she warned.

"Don't worry, I won't ask him for more personal details. For now."

Pip looked from Billie to me and then back to Billie.

"I promise I'll behave," Billie said.

"Okay, but join me soon," Pip agreed, still looking slightly alarmed.

As Pip left, I looked at Billie, "Well? Shall we go?"

"Go where?"

"Given that you wanted to talk about something without Pip here, I assumed you'd want to talk alone?"

Billie laughed, "Alright, yes, you are correct. Let's go for a walk," she said, standing. "Bye!" She waved to the other women as we headed out the door.

They didn't look confused at all by the events. Perhaps they were all in on something I wasn't. Now I was even more worried about whatever Billie wanted to speak with me about. As we walked down the path that wound its way around the edge of the village, Billie didn't make me wait long.

"So, I know you have some surprises in store for Piper—"

"How do you know?" I whispered as if Piper were somehow going to sneak up behind us.

"She knows," Billie said simply. "She doesn't know what the surprise is, but she knows you're planning something. Just like I am sure you know she is planning something. It's almost as if you were made for each other."

I crossed my arms and tried to scowl at her, but she was undeterred.

"It's fine, it's fine. Both of you love each other enough that you aren't going to ruin each other's surprises."

"So you took me on a walk to tell me we are both terrible secret keepers?" I huffed.

"No. I took you on a walk to suggest another secret," she said, still grinning.

She had my attention.

"Oh?"

"Well, Piper and I talked a bit about the orkin mating customs."

"Oh gods." I dragged my palm over my face.

"No, no, this isn't going where you think it is."

"It isn't?"

"No. We talked about how you didn't get to do any of the *Earth* customs," she explained.

"What kind of Earth customs?"

"Has she explained the concept of a wedding to you?"

I thought back on all the conversations Piper and I'd had about her life on Earth, "No, I don't think so."

"Okay, so in an American wedding, well I guess it would be any Western wedding, I think? But we're all American so we'll stick with what I know. Sorry, I'm rambling. I never thought I would have to explain a wedding to an alien." Billie paused seeing the very confused look on my face.

"Let's try again. In an American wedding the bride—

Piper, and the groom—you, stand up in front of all your family and friends and declare your commitment to each other. An officiant formally declares the union, and then the couple is announced as husband and wife. After, there is a party with dancing and cake."

"So you aren't asking me to mate with Piper in front of the entire tribe?" I asked.

I was even more confused because what she was asking seemed relatively simple. We regularly celebrated matings with a feast. This didn't seem too different, just a bit more formal.

"Holy fuck, no! Is that a thing here?" She looked horrified.

"No. We're a little freer with nudity than you all seem to be, but mating in front of the entire tribe would definitely be out of the norm."

"Why would you jump to that then?" she cried.

"I don't know! The way you were acting, I was expecting you to ask me to do something bizarre. This sounds just fine. Sure. Let's have an American wedding. But if Piper already knows about this, how would it surprise her?"

"Well, good sir. We haven't talked about an essential part that comes before the wedding. The proposal."

"Okay. What is a proposal?" I asked, growing concerned that this was where it would get weird.

"Well, generally, when it is a man and woman—male and female," she corrected, "the male gets down on one knee and lists all the reasons he loves his partner and then presents her with a ring and asks her to marry him."

"So you want me to ask her to marry me even though she has already agreed to be my mate for life?" I asked, confused.

"Yes," she said.

"Why would I ask if I already know she will say yes? Shouldn't we just start planning the wedding?"

"Because it's a thing!" she asserted. "Some people go over

the top crazy with proposals. They hire skywriters, set up elaborate scavenger hunts, or go on hot air balloon rides. I just gave you the simplest way it is usually done."

"Okay, I understood a minimal amount of what you just said. I don't even know what a balloon is, let alone a skywriter. But, putting that aside, you're saying that the actual act of asking Piper to marry me is a significant tradition?" I asked.

"Yes," she sighed.

"Alright."

"Alright, what?"

"Alright, I'll ask her. Why not? You'll need to help me set it up, but I can do that. Getting down on one knee and telling Piper why she's the perfect soul for me doesn't seem that hard," I said.

"Damn, she wasn't lying about you," she whispered to herself.

"Hmm?" I asked

"Oh, nothing, she just gushes about how wonderful you are," she said, rolling her eyes skyward.

I laughed, "Sorry, it doesn't seem like a large request now that I understand. Ask Piper to marry me. Have a wedding. Done."

"No concerns?" She didn't look convinced.

"Well, I will have to get a ring made. Magna made our best jewelry, but I think Skaard would be up to the task." I said, considering it, "When?"

"When?"

"Yes, when should I ask?" I repeated.

"Ah, that is for you to decide. But given that you are to be declared jarl and jarlin in two months, rolling the wedding into one big celebration makes sense. So, I would say sooner rather than later."

"Have you suggested combining our leadership change with a wedding to Piper?" I asked.

"No, I thought I'd let her think you came up with the idea, being excellent as it is and you being the perfect mate you are," she sassed.

I understood why Billie and Piper got along so well. Billie was talking to me just like Piper would.

"Well, I guess I need to head to the smithy. Is there any place in particular I should propose?"

"Someplace that is meaningful for both of you would be best," was all she said before she left me to formulate a plan.

CHAPTER 19

PIPER

*A*fter frantically working on multiple last-minute touches, moving day finally arrived for the human females. I'd spent the last couple of days splitting my time between helping the women pack up the meager belongings they had acquired since arriving and spending time with Osif's team and some of the other members of the tribe furnishing all of the women's rooms with the basics. With all the help we had, we planned to move everyone—including the displaced male orkin, all in one day. The entire tribe was all hands on deck.

I was on trip two of carrying belongings from one space to the next when I noticed a commotion up ahead at the new living quarters. Humans and orkin steadily moving in and out of spaces suddenly slowed. I watched as all eyes shifted to the edge of the village. I followed to where everyone was looking to see what could only be described as a nightmare.

Magna, or someone who appeared to be Magna, stood at

the front of a small group of orkin. He was so bruised and covered in what seemed to be a mixture of blood and mud, that it was hard to recognize him. The orkin behind him didn't look to be in any better physical condition. I saw what looked to be roughly splinted broken limbs, gashes covering body parts, and even what looked like a missing eye.

"Holy fuck," I breathed.

The air seemed to stand still as Magna stepped forward, limping and clearly putting in a great deal of effort to walk steadily. The tribe quietly split as Astrid rushed forward, followed closely by Agnarr.

"Hello, Magna. It looks as if you may have had a rough time," brow raised as she assessed him.

At this, Magna fell to his knees. A collective gasp rippled throughout the entire tribe.

"We've come to beg for your forgiveness. We have come to acknowledge the error of your ways. We have come to ask to be accepted back into the fold," Magna croaked, his voice sounding as rough as his appearance.

"And what has caused such drastic change in perspective?" Astrid asked.

"Well, we did not get very far on our journey before we were attacked by a pack of skogskatts at night. None of us are trained as guards and we naively thought we could protect ourselves. We didn't even think to set a night guard. They attacked on the third night of our journey. We lost two immediately. Almost all were injured. We sought shelter in a cave and stayed for several dagrs trying to nurse our most injured back to health. We lost another, but the rest were fit enough to continue."

"So being attacked by skogskatts convinced you that humans and females should be treated as equals?" she asked icily.

"No, no," he shook his head, "we attempted to continue

but were soon intercepted by a group of orkin from the Snaerfírar tribe on their way to trade with the Vátrfírar. They immediately provided us with aid and supplies, much to our surprise. However, things turned ugly once we explained why we were leaving Fýrifírar. Jarlin Piper was correct. Snaerfírar does have a half-orc amongst their tribe and they are fiercely protective of him. He was part of the group headed to Vátrfírar. He didn't want to see any bloodshed, but in my foolishness, I shared my thoughts on human women, and they attacked. We lost another male before Steve intervened. His tribe was furious and refused to take us in, but they did allow Steve to explain his position and how his mother came to be a part of their tribe. He advised that we make amends. It has taken us nearly a vika to get back to Fýrifírar," Magna finished and slumped back on his knees, clearly exhausted.

Astrid assessed the pathetic orc in front of her for a long moment.

"I cannot make this decision alone. It will be for the elders to decide," she said finally. "In the meantime, I am willing to see your injured are cared for—which appears to be all of you."

Astrid whipped her head around, looking through the tribe. As if on cue, one stepped forward.

"Emla, will you and Inga take them to your cabin? Do you have room for all of them?"

"Já, já, we can manage them all." She waved a hand dismissively, unfazed by all the injuries in a way only a seasoned healer would be. "I will need some help getting them all there, though."

Agnarr stepped forward, past Astrid and Emla, and held out a hand to Magna. His face was stony, but his hand remained out all the same. It was silent as Magna reached out and grabbed it, pulling himself up. I felt my eyes well up with tears, watching Agnarr extend such grace. Damn me for being such a crier.

The other orkin from Magna's group started to stumble forward. Some from the tribe approached to provide help. Ruby stepped around me and headed to the injured. I grabbed her arm to stop her.

"Ruby, you don't have to go," I hissed.

"I'm a nurse, and they are injured," she said, as if that settled it. "It is my duty to care for anyone who is injured, regardless of their prejudices," she carefully removed my hand from her arm and headed to one of the heavily limping orcs.

Ruby approached him and looped her arm around his waist, allowing him to lean on her despite their size difference. I watched, stunned, as they slowly shuffled toward Emla's cabin. If I wasn't crying before, I was definitely crying as I watched. Agnarr handed Magna off to another guard before approaching me. He pulled me into a rough embrace, causing me to drop the belongings I'd been carrying. I buried my face in his chest, taking a deep breath. I needed to steady myself before we continued.

I pulled away and quickly wiped my face before retrieving everything I'd dropped. I looked up to see Agnarr watching me, clearly concerned.

"This doesn't have to change anything," he said, so only I could hear. "We don't have to accept them back."

"Astrid's right. We should let the council decide—and we should bring Billie."

"Now?"

"Let me drop this off in Ginny's room. I'll find Billie, and we'll head to the longhouse. You find Astrid and the other elders and do the same? Tell Emla to leave the injured in Inga and Ruby's hands. With the whole tribe helping, the move can still go forward while we meet," I said.

"That sounds incredibly wise for someone who isn't even jarlin yet," Agnarr teased.

"I was a teacher for eight years. I'm always ready for a crisis," I said wearily then headed to Ginny's room.

I deposited Ginny's belongings on her new bed and then went to look for Billie. She was officially in charge of today's operations, so I knew she would be in the mix somewhere. It didn't take me long to spot her directing a group of adolescent orkin carrying pieces of furniture.

"Put whichever of them is most competent in charge. You need to come with me," I said.

Without missing a beat, she called out, "Thyra!" A young female orc carrying an entire dresser looked up. "Manage the team moving the furniture for the time being."

Thyra nodded without pausing.

"Ready?" she asked.

"You have them in line," I said, surprised.

"I helped manage a restaurant—I can manage a handful of teens. Who do you think makes up the majority of the hosts and servers? Kids under twenty."

"Fair. Let's go."

We headed to the longhouse, picking up Jodis, Alvis, and Bram along the way. When we arrived, we found the rest of the elders also approaching. As we sat and I looked around, I realized we were only missing one.

"Where is Skaard?" Agnarr asked, taking a seat to my right.

"He wouldn't come," Astrid said.

"He wouldn't come?" Agnarr asked, surprised.

"He said he didn't want his presence to impact our decision. I assured him it wouldn't, but he insisted, and we're on limited time. We need to get this going. The longer we wait for a decision, the more problems it will create. With everything in flux right now, adding an unstable group of would-be dissenters isn't ideal," Astrid explained.

"Okay, then let's put this to a vote first to see where everyone stands, then discuss," I stepped in.

Astrid looked surprised.

"There's no point in even hashing it out if we're all on the same page," I said.

"She does have a point," Agnarr murmured beside me.

Astrid shrugged in agreement, "Okay, a show of hands for those willing to let them stay?"

I looked around the room as eight hands went up, including my own—and, to my surprise, Billie's. That left only three not in favor of readmitting. I was even more surprised to realize those who hadn't raised their hands were Vigot, Astrid, and Agnarr.

"Well, we have a solid majority," Astrid said, "but a pretty clear division," looking at me with my hand up and Agnarr with his hand down. "I'm not voting for or against. It is too close to my departure for me to have sway here. I will stay and advise, but it will be up to our new leaders to determine how to proceed."

AGNARR

I was surprised that all the females voted to allow Magna and his followers to return—especially Piper and Billie.

"I don't want to put you two on the spot, but as you will be the most impacted if we allow Magna and his followers to return, I would like to hear from you," I said, directing myself toward Billie and Piper.

Billie spoke first, "Maybe I'm too trusting, but I believed him. Magna seemed changed."

"I've met Steve. It sounds accurate to how Steve would respond in a situation like that. And how the rest of his tribe would, as well. You remember how the Snaerfírar members treated him. He had a place of respect," Piper explained.

"I don't think he's lying about his experience. I am not certain I am ready to fully accept he had a change of heart," I replied.

"What if we put some expectations or parameters on their behavior? And some rules about how they are to act?" Runa suggested.

"And what would you suggest we do if they don't follow our rules?" Vigot asked.

"Then we kill them," Vott growled.

I wasn't surprised at Vott's response, given that he was head of the guard. But he had also voted to allow Magna and his group to return.

"Vott, if you want to kill them all, why did you vote to allow them to return?" I asked, rubbing my temples.

"I didn't say kill them all *now*. I said, kill them if they step out of line," Vott responded.

"Whoa, whoa, whoa," Piper leaned in, putting her hands up, "no one is killing anyone. I believe the option on the table is allowing them back in but having some requirements in place?"

"Yes, and I think that seems completely reasonable," Alvis, the elder charged with caring for the hestrs, agreed.

I looked around the table. Many heads were nodding.

"So we are in agreement that we are willing to let them return given that they follow some guidelines?" I asked.

"Uhhh, I think they should also pay some sort of penance," Billie piped up.

"Penance? This is a new word to me," I confessed.

"Like doing something to show they've changed. To atone — well, atone probably doesn't translate much better than penance—how about some sort of action to make amends?" she explained.

"I think that seems reasonable," I said.

Runa interjected with surprising fierceness, "No taking human mates!" she exclaimed.

I was astonished by the intensity coming from the tiny head cook. Though, I realized she spent much time with the human women. Many of them had chosen to help out in the kitchens as it was a primarily female space. She was probably very protective of them.

"No taking human mates, ever?" I clarified.

"How about no taking human mates, or even attempting to court the human women for at least one year?" Piper suggested diplomatically.

I looked around the room, more agreement.

"What about those that are too old to take mates? It looks like a couple of them lived—including Magna," Astrid asked, "how will they show... *penance?*"

"I am planning on adding a unit about humans and human culture for our orklings that are about to come of age to my classes. We could make them all take it. Ginny is planning to help me teach. I am sure Jarlin Piper would happily guest speak," Jodis, the elder of the teachers, suggested.

Piper laughed, "A few old males taking classes on human culture and customs with a bunch of teenagers? Sold!"

"And what if, after the ár, they haven't met the conditions we set forth? Or if they don't agree to the conditions at all?" Bram asked.

"Then they have to leave," Piper responded, much more seriously.

"But safely," Billie added, "Just because they aren't accepting of us doesn't mean we want them dead. And it's clear they won't make it to another tribe on their own."

"Really?" Vott questioned, incredulous.

"Must you always be so bloodthirsty?" I responded, exasperated.

"Comes with the territory," he said, giving me a grin that made him look almost boyish instead of a fearsome warrior.

I heard Piper and Billie giggling.

"Do not encourage him," I rolled my eyes skyward.

Piper composed herself and sat up straight.

"Okay, let me summarize. Magna and his remaining followers will be allowed to return on a conditional basis. The conditions are as follows: no one can take a mate, human or orc, for one year. All of them must take a class on human customs and traditions. They must agree to all of the conditions right now. If in a year the elders and the jarl and jarlin do not feel they have met the conditions and shown that they are changed, they will safely be escorted to another tribe. Does this all sound agreeable?"

I looked around to see heads nodding again. "Shall we put it to an official vote?"

"Já, já," numerous murmurs came from around the table.

"Okay, do we agree to let Magna and his supporters back into Fýrifírar if they agree to the conditions we provide them?"

All hands went up. Some were less enthusiastic than others, but all were up.

"What are your thoughts, Jarlin Astrid?" I asked.

"I think that Fýrifírar has a very bright future ahead of it with such a wise pair of leaders," she responded, giving me and Piper an approving smile.

Piper's face flushed, but she said nothing as she smiled back.

CHAPTER 20

PIPER

It was moving day. Again. This time I was hoping the day would prove to be less eventful. It was only Agnarr and I. After the disaster of moving day for the human women, we had very carefully chosen the team who would assist with our own process. Moving had always been a stressful thing for me. Even transitioning back home from college each summer caused such an upset to my nervous system that I waited days to unpack. I would unpack in the middle of the night, with a soothing baking show on in the background, slowly working to settle from one home to another.

Agnarr and I realized we would ruin many surprises we had in store for each other if we oversaw the furniture being installed, so we delegated to Osif and Billie. I'd grown incredibly fond of the grumpy old carpenter. The smell of wood shavings and sawdust that filled my nose when I entered Osif's workshop reminded me of my grandpa.

It had been a quiet week as the human women adjusted to their new space and the orkin males settled into their old rooms. Magna's group gladly accepted our conditions, with some of the older ones trying to hide back tears as we said we would allow them to return to their homes. Agnarr and I had shifted our focus to our own home. We spent many days apart, planning for different parts of the house. Neither of us were very good at keeping secrets.

I saw the tree and stump he had felled on me become a dining table, a mantel, and a beautiful enormous bed under Osif's skilled hands. Bram helped me pick out all our bedding and soft furnishings in the town center, guiding me to different merchants for everything needed to make a comfortable home. He even insisted on measuring me for a wardrobe. I'd had a few items made for me but I was basically living in the hand-me-downs that had been provided for all the women when we showed up. He insisted that as jarlin I should have a more expansive set of clothing options. I hoped that he'd listened to my request to keep it simple.

As I lay in bed, sifting through the events of the previous week, it took me longer than it should to realize Agnarr wasn't in bed with me. The sun was still low in the sky; it was much too early for him to be awake, let alone up and about. I loved my orc, and I loved that neither of us were morning people—beings? Whatever.

"Agnarr?" I called out, thinking maybe he was in the washroom.

No response.

I sat up and looked around. There was only one room. It wasn't like you could hide a giant lumbersnack. The fire crackled merrily, which meant Agnarr had added wood before he disappeared, and hadn't been gone long.

I sighed my displeasure that he had left without waking me.

I had grown used to waking up to find us tangled in each other.

I pulled back the covers and headed to our small shared dresser, growing oddly nostalgic that this would be our last night in his room together. Sure, I hadn't been here long, but it was technically the first place we lived together—unless a cave for the night counted.

I pulled on my borrowed leggings and a clean, but worn, tunic. I was glad I'd had boots made. It was so cold, having ones that fit correctly was important. I was just pulling my hair into a messy bun in the washroom when I heard the door open.

AGNARR

I walked into my room carrying a breakfast tray as Pip walked out of the bathroom wearing a frown. I thought she'd be happy I'd stoked the fire and retrieved breakfast before she woke up. She was usually up before me, but I knew she was on edge about moving.

"I brought breakfast," I said, setting the tray down on the table in front of the fire.

"You should have woken me," she grumbled. "Now I feel lazy."

Ah. This was a particular affliction of Pip's I'd come across. Her anxiety made it hard for her to rest. Even when she did rest, she felt guilty about it. I was learning she constantly needed to be assured she was doing more than her fair share of the work. I crossed the room and pulled her into my arms, all while she still had hers crossed over her chest, trapping her in my embrace. She squirmed, and I just held her to me, pressing my lips to her head and breathing in her scent.

"Pip, I had a couple of last-minute surprises to tie up. You have done more than your fair share of preparation. Honestly, you've done the majority of the work. I don't even know if we will have blankets or pots and pans," I reassured her while I stroked my fingers up and down her spine.

I felt her go loose and released her slightly, letting her maneuver her arms so they were around my waist, and she was able to look up at me.

"Yes, we have pots and pans. And blankets. And quite a few other things. Bram has been most insistent that our home be furnished with nothing but the best," she said, looking chagrined.

"Pip, no one in the tribe will judge us for having nice things. No one will think you demanded them. Look at what you're wearing," I said as I brushed a kiss to her nose.

"What's wrong with what I'm wearing?"

"Absolutely nothing, but it is not the outfit of a jarlin that demands special treatment."

"Fine, fine," she sighed, accepting my argument and leaning in to rest her head on my chest. "Are you ready?"

"More than ready."

"Well, then. Food. And then off we go."

I released her, and we both sat at the breakfast table. I watched as she helped herself to a small bowl of her favorite, gautr, and then added liberal amounts of dried fruit and syrup. I'd finally grown accustomed to how little she ate compared to me and stopped trying to stuff her full—well not of food anyway. I watched her take a scoop with a spoon and blow on it with her lovely pink lips. She was perfect.

Feeling my eyes on her, she looked up, "What?"

"Nothing, just admiring my beautiful mate," I said.

And soon-to-be fiance—if she said yes. And then my wife. Billie had explained these terms to me. She explained that being engaged was a special time for a couple. There were seemingly endless parties that went along with this whole

American wedding custom. She'd explained an engagement party, a bridal shower, bachelor party and bachelorette parties. It had left my head swimming. She assured me Pip probably wouldn't want all that, considering we were already mates, but I was ready to have seven hundred parties to celebrate our union if that's what Pip wanted.

I'd snuck off this morning to ensure everything about the *proposal* was set. I had to put a lot of trust in Billie and Osif because they wouldn't let me in the house, which was where I planned to propose. Billie told me she'd get flowers and ensure it looked perfect. While our customs seemed to vary quite significantly, it seemed an abundance of fresh flowers or greens at a celebration was something we shared.

Then I visited Magna. When they arrived, I knew the one thing that would convince me of his change of heart—an engagement ring. I knew Skaard would make a lovely ring once Billie thoroughly explained it, but I wanted Magna. He was the best. When I approached him with the idea, he was hesitant. He made it very clear that he was willing but wasn't sure how Pip would feel about wearing a ring made by him, given the way he'd treated her. I promised him it would signify his acceptance of her, and our new future. I had my directions from Billie—create something that made me think of Pip.

Magna had crafted a delicate gold band that mirrored the texture of wood grain—a nod to how we met, our future tribe, and Pip's love of trees. It was in a beautifully carved wooden box, thanks to Osif, and hidden in the pocket of my cloak. I absentmindedly wondered how human males kept their proposal secrets from their partners. I found it incredibly difficult, and it had only been a few vikas. Soon. Soon, there would be no more secrets. I shook myself and started to gather myself breakfast to find it was Pip's turn to stare at me.

"Where'd ya go there, buddy?" she teased

"Huh?" I blinked slowly.

"You just totally disappeared in thought for a good few minutes."

"Oh," I choked, blushing green, "just thinking—thinking about our future."

It wasn't a lie—technically.

"Yeah, I've been doing a lot of that too. Are you ready for this?" she asked.

I almost gave it away then and there, thinking she was asking me if I was ready for marriage, only to realize she was asking me if I was prepared to become jarl.

"Yes. I am. We are. We've been forged in fire. There is nothing we can't take on together," I asserted.

I was surprised to see Pip's eyes swimming with tears.

"What's wrong?" I left my food and kneeled in front of her.

She took my face in her hands and gave me a swift kiss, "Nothing, nothing at all. I just love you so much."

"I love you too," I whispered, kissing her.

"Okay, okay. We need to get a move on. Eat. I've seen how much you need to sustain your giant body. We have a busy day," she said, pushing me back and returning to her breakfast.

We ate in companionable silence. Soon, it was time. We gathered what we had packed from my room, which wasn't much. I was leaving behind the bedding and towels, knowing we'd have new things once we arrived. We had our clothes and a few other things. If we'd set everything up right, it would be a one-trip move.

It was still early, just as Pip had asked. She didn't want any fanfare for moving day. She said we'd save that for the day we took leadership. Moving gave her anxiety, so she wanted it to be just us as much as possible. I knew she'd met with Billie, Osif, and Bram multiple times, but she wanted this to be a just-us moment. I was happy to indulge her, knowing all the surprises I had in store. I couldn't hold her hand, given everything we were carrying, but I walked close enough to her that I could inhale her sweet scent. It wasn't long before we reached the short path off the main thoroughfare that encircled the tribe.

The path to our new home was lined with furutré before opening up to a little clearing with our house sitting in the middle, the forest rising in the back. The outside of the house had been overgrown, the prior owner having passed long ago. The brush had been cleared, and the front of the house scrubbed clean. They even replaced the roof after we went back and forth about how long it would last. Osif had ultimately decided on a new one. From the outside, the house looked brand new. I hurried ahead of Pip to open the door for her. We hadn't seen the inside in weeks, Billie and Osif keeping it strictly off limits. I ushered Pip in and followed closely behind her.

PIPER

I held my breath as I walked into our new home. I had no idea what to expect. I knew the house's layout but hadn't been inside since they started working on it. I walked into the great room to find a fire already burning merrily, a brand new mantelpiece above it. I grinned, thinking of the conversation I'd had with Osif. In front of the fireplace was a huge sofa that I had picked out with Bram. To the right of it was a round dining table with intricately carved legs that stood just like the mantlepiece. I brushed my fingers across it before looking back at Agnarr.

"What do you think of the new furniture?"

"It's beautiful," Agnarr said as he approached the table.

"It's your tree—or our tree, rather," I explained.

"Our tree?" He looked confused.

"Yes, the tree where we met," I said, beaming at him.

"Oh gods, Pip," he said, covering his hand with his face, failing to hide the dark green of embarrassment creeping up his neck.

"You don't like it? It's where we started our relationship!" I laughed, enjoying teasing him, "It was only appropriate to be in our home."

Agnarr looked at me, clearly torn between embarrassment and amusement.

"You look at the disastrous tree incident as the beginning of our relationship?" he finally asked.

"Well, it's how we first met, and though it didn't start very well, I felt like it ended spectacularly," I said, smiling.

"Okay, I'll allow it. But our dining table?"

"And the mantle. And our bed. It seemed only fitting," still smiling, completely unrepentant.

Agnarr placed the parcels he'd been carrying on the table and pulled me into a fierce hug.

"Oh, Pip, my fiery little mate. It *is* fitting," he murmured before releasing me, "But can it be our secret?"

"Um, only if *our* includes Billie and Osif... and probably the rest of the women?"

"You truly show no mercy, my mate," he said, resigned.

"Nope. None at all," I said, kissing him again. "Shall we look around?" I asked.

We looked over the kitchen together. It was basic, as we knew we'd be eating most meals with the tribe, but it had everything we needed should we decide we needed some time away. Looking around the rest of the great room, there were hooks by the front door, and what looked almost like a human shoe rack, if not significantly larger—finally, the first closed door. I knew everything that was inside it, but Agnarr didn't. I'd watched Osif design and build the desk and chairs, as well as the beginnings of what would become several built-in bookcases. I picked out soft rugs and oil lamps with Bram. I was itching with anticipation to show Agnarr his new office as jarl.

"Let's see what they decided to do with this room," I said, pulling the door open and walking in.

Billie, Osif, and Bram did not disappoint. The room was dominated by a giant, beautiful wooden desk with a lit oil lamp sitting on it. I wondered how early Billie and Osif had gotten up to ensure the entire house was lit up. Bookshelves were built into the wall on either side of the desk, and two squishy-looking chairs in opposite corners looked like lovely places to curl up and read.

"Well, do you like your office?" I asked.

"You did this for me?" Agnarr looked stunned.

"Of course. The jarl needs a place to meet with his tribe members. What if someone wants to speak with you about an issue or a dispute? Or if you need to write letters to other tribes. You need a space," I explained.

I watched Agnarr walk around the room, admiring all the extra touches I'd added, ensuring the space was comfortable for long work hours. He sat down at the carved chair at his desk before gliding his hand across its top.

"This isn't... um... our tree, is it?" he asked, looking pointedly at the desk.

"No, no, it isn't. I thought you'd want to keep that out of your office. Though," I said upon further examination of the height and width of the desk, "perhaps not?" voice hitching.

"Hmm... there's some potential there," he said, eyeing me. "But we have other rooms to look at."

We left his office, and I was surprised to realize there was a new door on the wall just before the stairs.

"Did you have them add another door? Why?"

"Yes, Pip. I had them add another door. To nowhere. Just a door," Agnarr said, voice dripping with sarcasm.

"Alright, alright. I knew we both had surprises. I just didn't expect—Well, I don't know what I expected," I huffed.

"Maybe you should open the door?"

I rolled my eyes but opened the door all the same. I don't know what I expected, but it wasn't what I found. Agnarr had them add on an entire room. A whole ass room. I was no carpenter, but my brain couldn't really wrap itself around how there was no room here before, and now there was one. I decided not to think about it too much. The room was pretty spacious but had seating everywhere, all overstuffed and cozy looking, from armchairs to little padded poufs. It was brightly colored and felt warm and welcoming.

"What is this room for?" I asked, admiring it.

"Count the seating."

"Huh?"

"Count the seating."

I quickly counted all the chairs, poufs, and cushions. Twelve. There were twelve places to sit comfortably. Dammit, my eyes started to well up. If I were going to be mated to someone this sweet, the waterworks would never stop.

"You made a room for me and all the women?" I cried.

"They'll want to see you often. And *I* want to see you often. This way, you don't have to go to them. They have a place they can feel comfortable here," he said as if it were some simple thing.

I wrapped myself around him, squeezing with all my might, "It's perfect. Thank you."

Agnarr wrapped me up in his arms, kissing me from the top of my head down to my cheek and settling where my neck met my shoulder.

"No more surprises, though, right? I already told you about all of mine. I don't want to be a crying mess all day,"

Agnarr looked almost remorseful as he scooped me up bridal style and carried me out of the room. I yelped in surprise.

"I'm terribly sorry, Pip, but I have one more surprise," he said, voice low, as he carried me up the stairs.

CHAPTER 21

AGNARR

I carried Pip up the stairs toward the largest bedroom in the back. Having not seen anywhere else in the house set up for a proposal, I knew Billie must have done it in our bedroom. Excellent choice, given that it was taking all I could not to bend Piper over my new desk and fuck her senseless. Lovely as the desk was, the sentiment behind it was far more touching. Pip had put so much thought into what I would need to lead. I smiled down at her.

"Agnarr, if you are taking me upstairs to fuck me in our new bed, that's not a surprise," she said, meeting my gaze. She was trying to figure out what else I had planned.

"What makes you think I want to fuck you in our new bed?"

"Well. First, you always want to fuck me. Second, we haven't had sex in like three days because we've been so busy. I expect you are crawling out of our skin like I am. Third, it's our new bed."

I stifled a laugh, "These are all solid points. And yes, I would like to fuck you in our new bed. I hope you thought to get several bedding sets because I plan to make a mess of you. But no, that is not what the surprise is."

She squinted up at me, and I looked straight ahead. I was determined to make it to our new bedroom without telling her. I reached our door and twisted the knob while still holding her in my arms. I pushed it open and found Billie had outdone herself.

There were candles everywhere. They lit a table on either side of our bed, sat flickering in a neat row on the mantle of our second fireplace, and in a beautiful candelabra on a low table in front of it. She'd arranged winter greenery in the empty spaces, bunching it into beautiful displays that made the red berries that grew in the snow almost glow in the candlelight. I knew I only had a moment before everything clicked into place for Piper.

I let go enough for her to find her feet and took a knee before her. I couldn't help but feel a bit foolish, but choosing to believe Billie, I grasped Pip's hands. Her mouth hanging open in shock was enough to tell me I was on the right track. She looked at me, stunned.

"Agnarr, wha— what?"

I'd practiced this many times. I had to get it right the first time.

"Piper, I know I am not who you expected for a partner. I know I went about our relationship in a way that is entirely foreign to you. But I want you to know that I love you with all that I am. You challenge me and make me strive to be the best version of myself. I want to be that orc for you and you alone. I want to be by your side when you wake each morning and hold you every night as you fall asleep. I don't just want to be your mate. I want to be your husband. I want to build a life and a family together and rule together, side by side. Will you do me the honor of becoming my wife? Will you marry me and allow me to love you for the rest of our lives?"

I pulled the ring box out of my cloak pocket and opened it in front of Piper.

Pip's mouth opened and closed and opened again. I'd rendered her speechless.

"Pip, I think this is where you are supposed to answer me."

"Agnarr, you didn't have to—we don't have to—" she stammered.

I interrupted her, "Oh, but I did. And we do. So will you? Will you marry me?"

"Ye—yes, yes. Yes," she said before falling to her knees and wrapping herself around me, completely ignoring the ring in my hand and pulling me in for a kiss.

I attempted to make it a brief press of our lips so I could put the ring on her finger and finish the proposal properly, but Piper had none of it. She slid her hands into my hair and tugged at my lower lip with her teeth. I opened for her, letting her small, soft tongue invade my mouth. She stroked her tongue against mine, sliding it up and down. The feel and taste of her were an onslaught to my senses.

The ring would have to wait. I set the box on the floor and grabbed Piper by the waist, pulling her closer to me. I needed more of her. I pulled at the bottom of her tunic, attempting to take it off, but she stopped me.

"Do you remember what I wanted when we first met? When you felled that stupid tree on me?" she asked, reaching for the laces in my leather pants.

"You wanted... um... you wanted—" She was expecting me to think now? With my mind in complete disarray at the smell of her arousal and the feel of her yanking my pants down.

"I wanted you to fuck me—and you wouldn't. Because you said you wanted it to be more than just a casual fuck in the woods."

She wrapped her hand around the base of my cock, giving it a firm tug. All control I'd had of the situation completely vanished.

"Well, now it isn't some casual fuck in the woods. I want you to fuck me like you and I both knew we wanted to then," she pumped me up and down, leaning her forehead against mine.

I tried to gather my thoughts. I'd expected this to be one of our more sensual lovemaking sessions, given the candles and the proposal, but here Pip was, again, completely surprising me.

"Pip, if you don't stop that, I won't be able to fuck you at all," I groaned as she continued to work my shaft.

She released me. I stood, pulling her up as she wrapped her arms around my neck and legs around my waist, all while kissing up my neck and along my jaw. I stood trapped, with my pants half down and my new fiancee attempting to devour me with enthusiasm.

I pulled back, "If we are going to make it to the bed, you need to let me get my pants all the way off."

She stopped the open mouth kisses she was pressing against the sensitive skin behind my ear reluctantly and let me go. She looked at me mischievously before quickly shucking her boots and her pants, leaving her in nothing but the tunic that barely covered her ass and cunt. I was nearly drooling at the sight of her rounded cheeks as she walked to our bed. *Our bed.* She was right. It was an excellent bed. Large, with four posters and an expanse of soft gray bedding.

I finished stripping and joined her. Pip moaned as I settled my larger body over hers, letting her scent envelop me like a drug. I wanted to be everywhere at once.

"Hello, my sweet Pip," kiss, "my mate," kiss, "my fiancée," I punctuated each statement with a bruising kiss, leaving Pip panting and writhing under me.

"Fiancée, eh?" She grinned.

"You did say yes. Am I mixing up how this works?" I asked, acting clueless on purpose.

"Yes, that is how this works. We are engaged," she laughed. "I'm engaged to my fated orc mate. Sure, that makes sense."

"Enough talking. I thought you wanted me to fuck you like I wanted to that first day," I kissed her again, this time pulling her lips apart and delving into her mouth deeply, stroking my ridged tongue into her soft mouth. I thrust my tongue in and out in a way that had her moaning and squirming beneath me. I left her lips and kissed down her neck and across her collarbone, along the edge of her tunic. Kissing down her chest, I felt her nipples harden beneath the thin fabric. I licked and sucked each of them, leaving wet patches in my wake as I continued down her torso.

Pip moaned and grabbed my head, panting, "I asked you to fuck me like you wanted to, not torture me."

I shoved Pip's tunic up, exposing her breasts, before licking across her hipbone, "Off with it," I growled. "I think, if you remember correctly, that this is what I wanted to do that first day we met."

I spread her wide roughly, in a way I knew she liked, throwing one leg over each of my shoulders. I licked the entire length of her wet heat, pausing to circle my tongue around her clit. Pip let out a choked scream as I continued to lick her up and down before returning to suck gently on her clit. I may have wanted to do something like this the day we first met, but now I knew exactly what she liked. I knew that when her hands tightened in my hair and her thighs started shaking, she was close and that I should keep the same pace and pressure to see her over the edge.

I continued the same rhythm of steady licking and sucking, driving Pip higher and higher. With a final gasp, she clamped her thighs down around me and shattered beneath me. I continued my ministrations until her legs went limp, and she loosened her grip on my hair.

As tempting as it was to give her a moment of reprieve, I knew what Pip asked for. Watching her come apart under my tongue made me desperate to hammer into her precisely the way she'd demanded. I only glimpsed her wide eyes before I lifted her legs off my shoulders and flipped her beneath me, pulling her up onto her knees by her hips.

I massaged her perfect ass as I spread her legs wide. She looked back at me, eyes hungry, one eyebrow raised. "Well?"

I used one hand to push her chest down onto the bed and my other to notch my dripping cock at her entrance. I felt her breath catch as I thrust into her in one fluid movement. We both groaned as I bottomed out inside her. Though we'd now fucked countless times—enough for me to know that this was her favorite position—it was incomparable every time. Maybe it was Pip, perhaps it was the mate bond, but nothing had ever felt this good. I gave her just a moment to adjust to me before pulling back and beginning to thrust into her with steady, deep strokes.

"Oh fuck, how do you feel this good?" she panted.

"Because you are mine; this cunt was made for me." I'd never let my more aggressive side out with any other partner, but Pip craved it. She wanted to lose control, and I was happy to take it. Ratcheting up my pace as I curled my body over hers, I kissed down her neck. I used one hand to massage her breast and pinch her nipple before reaching down to find her clit. I almost came at the feeling of my cock sliding in and out of her, but I wanted one more orgasm out of her first. As I thrust into her again, I pressed down on her clit with the pad of my thumb, just enough for her to come apart.

Pip let out an unintelligible string of words as I felt her clamp down on me, milking my cock with her climax. Her orgasm spurred me even more. It was one, two, three thrusts , then I joined her over the edge, climaxing with such force that stars swam in my vision. I shifted to the side as I toppled forward so I wouldn't smother her with my body. Instead, pulling her into the spooning position she was so fond of. We lay in silence, our breath evening out, pulses slowing. Pip reached back and stroked my arm, giving out a contented sigh. I pulled her in close to me, wrapping my arms around her.

"I love you, my fiancée," I whispered into her ear.

PIPER

Fiancée. I was in utter bliss, coming down from the high of being fucked boneless by Agnarr. My fiancé. I knew he'd planned surprises for our first day, but I hadn't expected a proposal. I hadn't given the conversation with Billie a second thought, too many things were happening. It was down the road, something for after everything settled down. I did want a wedding eventually. I never thought I'd get a proposal. I already had a fated mate. That he got down on one knee and asked me to marry him on top of everything was almost too much. We spooned on our new bed in the quiet of the morning.

"So what now?" I stroked the arm he'd wrapped around me.

"What do you want to do now?"

"I'm perfectly fine to do this for now. We've been rushing for days. I could lay here in your arms for quite some time," I pulled his arm tighter around me until I felt completely surrounded.

"Then that's what we will do."

"You know, you didn't have to ask me to marry you. I know that isn't something you do here."

"I know. But it is something you do back on Earth. You shouldn't give up all of your customs for me. I want to be your mate and your fiancé. Eventually, your mate and your husband."

The term husband sounded so weird coming from Agnarr. I laughed.

"What?" He sounded affronted, "I can't be your husband?"

"Yes, yes," I laughed even as I placated him, "I want you to be my husband, but it makes me laugh because you are already so much more than a husband."

"How so?"

"Well," I explained, "husband and wife are meant to be permanent, but they often aren't. Loads of couples get divorced."

"Divorced?" It was clear he'd never said the word.

"Yeah. They end their relationship. People grow apart, fall out of love, or meet someone else. I told you about my parents. Though, with them, I'm not sure they were ever in love."

"That's... I don't like that," Agnarr grumbled as if the mere thought of separating pained him. It pained me, too. His knot had softened enough for me to slip off him and roll so I could see him. I wanted to see his face and to reassure him.

I looked into his dark brown eyes, "Well then, let's not talk about it because that's not us. We will never get divorced or separate. We're lucky. I'm lucky," I wrapped myself around him and sighed into his warm body. I truly could stay like this forever.

CHAPTER 22

Piper

I wanted to stay in Agnarr's arms and rest in our new bed, but his substantial amount of cum was becoming increasingly apparent as it cooled. I mentally thanked Bram for insisting on four sets of bedding. "Love?" I asked.

"Mmm?"

"Is there a washroom up here?"

"Já, we have one connected to our bedroom up here, and the full sauna is downstairs."

I scooted away from Agnarr, but he locked his arms around me, kissing my head, "You aren't going anywhere."

"I just want to clean up. And maybe put on some fresh bedding. If you hadn't noticed, we've made a mess."

"We have, but I want to finish this proposal before you go anywhere," he released me and stood, looking for something at the foot of the bed. When he returned, he had a small, ornately carved wooden box in his hand. I recognized Osif's work immediately.

"What's this?" I asked though I was already pretty sure what I would find inside.

"Open it, and maybe you will find out," he said, laying back down beside me.

Opening the box, I wasn't surprised to find a ring. I *was* surprised by the design. It mimicked the bark of the trees that surrounded our cabin and covered the forest. It was so intricately made I couldn't believe it wasn't made of tree bark, taken down to a small, delicate scale. Agnarr took the ring and slipped it on my ring finger. I held my hand out to admire it. The gold sparkled in the candlelight. It was nothing like I would have picked for myself, but it was perfect.

"Do you like it?"

"I love it. Did Skaard make it?"

"No. Magna did."

"Seriously?" I pulled my hand closer to my face to inspect the detail further.

"Seriously," Agnarr responded, teasing.

"I just wouldn't think that Magna would be willing to make something like this for me, given everything that has happened," I said, still inspecting the ring.

"At first, he didn't want to. He told me to ask Skaard. Magna didn't think you would wear a ring made by him. Skaard would have done beautiful work, but Magna's work is better. And I wanted it to be a symbol not just of our love but of our future as a tribe, orkin and human side-by-side."

"Is that all?" I rolled my eyes.

Agnarr huffed, "*And* I knew if Magna really hadn't changed his mind about learning to accept the humans, he would never agree to make it. So it was a bit of a test for him."

"That is a lot of meaning behind a tiny gold band," I teased.

"Do you still want to wear it, even though Magna made it?"

"I'll consider it," I said blithely while still inspecting the intricacies of the carved metal. "Are you going to wear one as well?"

"Do you want me to wear one?"

"Back home, both partners do. It is a symbol of our commitment. I know we both bear a much more permanent sign down our spines, but... yeah, I want you to wear one too. Maybe one that's a little manlier."

"Manlier?" Agnarr looked confused.

"I mean, less dainty," I clarified. "Something this delicate would look silly on your giant hands."

"Ah, okay. I will talk to Magna tomorrow. We will have a matching pair. Billie said sometimes you get a second band on the wedding day. Do you want a second band?"

"Nope, I like this one. I'll have to give it back to you before the wedding so we can officially put them on during the ceremony, but I am keeping it for now," I beamed up at Agnarr, "But, can we please go get clean now? I am cold and sticky."

Agnarr just laughed as he stood to lead me down to the sauna.

AGNARR

It had been two vikas since Piper and I had moved into our new home. We were settled. The other women visited regularly, and we stopped getting our meals delivered, instead joining the longhouse for meal times. We wanted to be present as much as possible. There were only a few days left before the double ceremony: an American wedding and the celebration of a new jarl and jarlin. We'd also extended invitations to the entire tribe, wanting everyone to feel welcome to knock on our door. Many had taken us up on the offer.

It felt again as if we were preparing for something monumental. I hoped after this last ceremony and celebration, we could end the winter quietly, with Pip and I getting to spend quiet evenings together in front of our fireplace—or in bed. I was on my way to visit Bram for a last fitting of the new tunic and pants Piper insisted I have made. Though I pretended to object, wanting her to be the focal point that day, deep down, I was touched by her thoughtfulness. In truth, I would have shown up naked if it pleased her. But I wanted the day to be about Piper, so I would dress in whatever finery she desired.

As I entered Bram's workshop, the aging tailor smiled at me from his sewing.

"Ah, Jarl Agnarr," he beamed.

"No, no, not yet. And not ever. I will always be just Agnarr," I said genially. I didn't want anyone to feel as though I held myself above them. We were all part of the same tribe. The formality of being addressed by my new title chafed at me.

"Já, já, if you insist." Bram hardly paid attention to me as he laid out my tunic and pants.

I shucked my clothing and carefully pulled on the garments, not wanting to damage or wrinkle them. I looked at myself in the full-length mirror and was happy with the outcome. My tunic was light blue with intricate gold embroidery along the hems. My pants were fairly standard leather, but brand new and a nice warm brown. They would go well with my new boots. I held my arms in front of Bram, silently asking his opinion.

"Já, your outfit will complement Jarlin Piper's gown perfectly. It is done," he motioned for me to take it off.

I pulled the tunic over my head and removed the pants,

handing both to him as I put my clothing back on. Bram neatly packaged the clothes before passing them to me.

"Please remind Brandr that he must also attend a last fitting?" Bram asked as I took the parcel.

I sighed, "I will try. Brandr likes finery even less than I do and doesn't have the same interests I have in making Pip a pleased mate."

"Oh, I am well aware," Bram drolled. "Perhaps you could have Jarlin Piper convince him?"

I laughed, "That isn't a bad idea. Thank you for these. I would attempt to pay you, but I don't need to be shouted at again."

"No, you do not."

I waved as I exited his shop, still laughing to myself. When Piper explained the concept of a maid of honor and best man, I was slightly confused, but it didn't take long to understand. Who wouldn't want their best friend beside them as they made one of the most important commitments of their life? Brandr was a straightforward choice. He and I had been friends since we were orklings. It also meant I didn't have to choose between my two brothers. Piper, unsurprisingly, picked Billie to be her maid of honor.

Adding the wedding to the ceremony was fairly simple because preparations for the transition of power were already in motion. We'd asked Astrid to officiate the ceremony. Once Piper explained what the position entailed, Astrid agreed readily. She even suggested that she wrap the wedding ceremony into the announcement of us as the new leaders. Runa had been delighted to prepare for another feast. Feeding others brought her nothing but joy. Bram had brought together some other business leaders and humans to decorate the longhouse. I knew Astrid's love of plants would be displayed everywhere in the decor.

I meandered my way back to our house, wondering if I

should stop by Brandr's house to push him into getting fitted, but decided to let Piper have at him, or better yet, Billie. I thought Piper was stubborn. But when Billie wanted something accomplished on behalf of her best friend, she was a force of nature. Yes, Billie would be the right person to march Brandr to his fitting. Decision made, I picked up the pace, hoping to catch Piper before she headed to the longhouse for the midday meal. She and several of the women were in the house when I left this morning. Pip told me they were talking about decor as she kissed me goodbye, but they were giggling far too much to be talking about greenery and candles. I was confident they all knew far too many intimate details about our sex life.

PIPER

The wedding was three days away, and I was calm. Too calm. I was so calm about it, I was trying to come up with things to be anxious about. *Thanks, anxiety.* I sat in the quiet of midmorning and sipped an extra cup of baldrian tea, trying to think of something to worry about. I came up with nothing. I wondered if I would be this calm if I were having a wedding back on Earth. I nixed that as even a possibility. If I were having a wedding back on Earth, my family would be involved. Suddenly, I was delighted to have been abducted by aliens.

I sipped tea as I sat in Agnarr's study, waiting for him to return from his fitting. I'd had my final fitting the previous day. Like everything about my life now, my wedding dress was nothing like I would have envisioned, but it was perfect. Given the winter snow and the cold, it was long-sleeved and looked almost conservative from the front. Bram embroidered the hems and sleeves with intricate gold details that shimmered in the light. But it was the back of the dress that made it stunning. I wanted to acknowledge that Agnarr and I were more than just husband and wife. We were Elska mates. I wanted to show off my mating marks.

Bram, understanding my vision, had cut an almost dangerously low back that would display my marks for all to see as I walked down the aisle. He seemed to think it odd but was happy with the outcome. I was keeping the details of the dress from Agnarr. I knew he'd get one look at it and haul me over his shoulder back to our bed.

I was staring out the window, mind adrift, when I heard our front door open. I rushed to greet Agnarr and had myself wrapped around him before he could even remove his cloak. I peppered his neck and jaw with kisses as he attempted to set down his package. Agnarr laughed and slipped out of my grasp to remove his cloak and set everything down.

"I take it you missed me?" He returned to embrace me.

"Mmm, of course, I missed you." I looped my arms around his neck and pulled him down for a kiss.

"You seemed pretty happy with the women when I left. What were you all giggling about?"

"Oh, we were just discussing an American wedding tradition that I don't think you will be very fond of," I grinned at him. I had been explaining these traditions as *American* traditions, even though I knew most of them spanned several countries. I was ignorant of everything non-western, so I tried to stick with what I knew.

"Was it the one where I stick my head under your dress in front of everyone? Because I thought we already agreed you didn't want to do that one," he grimaced.

"No, no," I laughed, "Definitely no garter toss. I wouldn't have done that even if we were still on Earth. It's always weirded me out."

Agnarr looked relieved, "Okay then, what's this one?"

"Well, usually, the bride and groom spend the evening

apart the night before the wedding," I looked at him uncertainly, knowing he wouldn't be a fan.

"No. Why? Why would you be apart from me?" He looked almost pained at the suggestion.

Deciding now was not the time to explain virginity and all the garbage that went along with it; I went for the more modern explanation. "It is to heighten the surprise and excitement of the wedding day. You aren't supposed to see me in my wedding dress until the ceremony, so I can hardly get ready with you," I explained.

"What if you need me?" he asked, eyebrows raised, making his meaning clear.

"That's kind of the point. Wedding night sex is supposed to be amazing and memorable. I mean, it rarely is because half the time, the couple is too exhausted or drunk even to have sex, but that's the tradition."

"Ah, so we don't have sex the night before the wedding to make the wedding night sex better? Because we've gone without?" He was catching the idea, at least somewhat.

"Yes, exactly," relieved he followed.

"No. I don't think that will work," Agnarr said, crossing his arms over his chest.

"What? Why not? It is a tradition I want to do—mainly for the surprise factor. And think of how amazing sex will be if we've been apart," I batted my eyelashes at him. He looked down at me, and I could tell his resolve was crumbling.

"What if you get hurt?"

"How will I get hurt spending the night in Billie's room? That's not even a good argument."

"No, no, definitely not. If we are doing this at all, you will stay here. I will sleep elsewhere," he sighed.

"So we can do this?" I asked, already knowing the answer.

"You know I would never actually say no to something you wanted. Especially considering all the customs you've endured assimilating into our culture. But that doesn't mean I have to like it. And I am stationing a guard outside. And I want all the women here. You can make it like that bachelorette thing Billie explained to me," he said darkly, like the women were taking me from him.

"That sounds amazing. Could I make it up to you? To thank you for putting up with a silly tradition?"

"What did you have in mind?"

"Well, if you aren't busy right now..." I reached out and trailed a finger down his chest.

Agnarr said nothing as he lifted me and swung me over his shoulder, heading for the stairs.

"For the millionth time, I can walk!" I protested.

"Já, but this is faster."

CHAPTER 23

PIPER

The morning of our wedding day dawned bright and crisp. I felt refreshed, thanks to Zoey. While I was still getting to know the petite blonde, she had a military background and insisted on an early bedtime for all of us. I wasn't sure where we would all sleep, but all 'the girls,' as I'd affectionately started calling them, showed up with blankets and pillows. It really was going to be like a giant sleepover. Since my group of friends had always been on the smaller side back on Earth, having a built-in set of eleven friends was a little overwhelming. But I took it in stride and tried to push aside my social anxieties as we chatted and snacked throughout the evening. I tried on my dress for everyone. They oohed and ahhed appropriately.

We tried to play a game of truth or dare, but since no one was willing to go out in the cold, no dares were taken. It ended up being an evening of deep talk about what our lives had been and where they were going. While some of the girls were still scared of the future, many were ready to move forward and solidify their space in Fýrifírar. I, more than anyone, was prepared for the future. After today, I wanted a bit of quiet. Less ceremonies and celebrations, more sleeping in, and lazy afternoons. One tradition Agnarr hadn't fought me on at all was a honeymoon. With us taking control of the tribe, it couldn't be a long one, but we agreed to three days back at the ceremonial pools, and I was probably more excited about that than I was about the wedding.

As I started shuffling around the rest of the girls woke up and joined me in the kitchen. Quite a few of them drank Baldrian tea, so I made an entire pot rather than the usual cup I made for myself. A soft knock came at the door, and there stood Tora and Odin, carrying heavy trays of breakfast. I hurried them in so they could place the trays down on the dining table before pulling them both into an awkward group hug where we were both laughing and hugging little Odin's head. Even though it had only been a few months, he seemed taller.

"Have your tusks grown since I last saw you?" I gasped in mock astonishment.

"Jarlin Piper, you just saw me last vika," Odin responded very seriously.

I laughed, "I remember. And I remember telling you to call me Piper. Do you call Astrid Jarlin Astrid?"

"No, but that's because I call her Aunt Astrid," he giggled.

"Well, do you think you can try to call me Piper?" I asked.

He gave Tora a suspicious look before nodding and heading to the breakfast trays.

"Leave some for the women," Tora admonished him as he grabbed three pastries, "you've already had breakfast."

"Don't worry about it. He can have my share. I'm not very hungry. I will have a bowl of gautr," I assured Tora.

"Nervous?" she asked knowingly.

"Mmm, not about marrying Agnarr. He's mine for keeps already. I don't think I am nervous about becoming jarlin. I think I am most worried about having to be social for an entire day. It's exhausting."

"Take breaks. You know anyone in this room would manage things if you stepped out of the longhouse to get some fresh air. Just don't go running off to the woods again?" she teased.

"I have no reason to run off to the woods. Everything I want is right here," I said, welling up at the enormity of acknowledging it.

Everything I wanted was here.

AGNARR

I tried not to feel awkward as I stood alone next to a very significant tree stump. Piper asked me to meet her here before the ceremony. It felt like I had been waiting for ages, but it was just nerves. I'd been there mere moments when Piper appeared, heading for me. She was a vision in her finery. Her long cream-colored gown looked buttery soft and had embroidery that matched my own. She wore a deep blue cloak and had her hair intricately braided with winter greenery woven throughout. There was something different about her face that I couldn't quite put my finger on. As she got closer, I realized her eyelids had a sparkle to them, and her lips were a much richer shade of pink than I was used to. She must have read the puzzled look on my face.

"It's just makeup."

"Makeup?"

"Paint that humans sometimes put on their faces? I used to wear it back on Earth. I usually wore some for special occasions. Today counts as a special occasion. Tora said that sometimes orkin women line their eyes for special ceremonies."

"Does it come off?"

"Yes, it comes off. Do you not like it?" She looked concerned.

"You look stunning, but I prefer your face without paint." Apparently, this was the right thing to say because it earned me a giant smile.

"Would you like to see the dress?"

"It is amazing," I responded, admiring the detail up close. It hugged Piper's curves beautifully. She unclasped her cloak and laid it on the stump, turning her back to me.

I knew nothing about female clothing, but the back of Piper's dress was more than I was ready for. It wasn't a back as much as it was a *lack* of a back. It cut in such a deep v that it stopped just above the swell of her ass. The back of the dress perfectly highlighted the mating marks etched down Piper's spine. I didn't say anything. I didn't even breathe as I traced the patterns with one gentle finger.

"I'll take it you like it?" Piper looked over her shoulder at me.

I wrapped my arms around her and pulled her against my chest, pressing kisses down her exposed neck. "Hey, hey, careful of the hair," she pulled away and turned to face me.

"It is perfect. No one will doubt our status as a mated pair, human or orkin. Is this why you wanted to see me before the ceremony?"

"Yes. You won't see the back as I walk down the aisle to you. I wanted you to be the first to see it."

I tried to pull her in for a kiss, but she stopped me, pushing against my chest with her hands. "Ah, not before the ceremony. And you'll ruin my lipstick."

"You show up here in that dress, and I'm not allowed to kiss you?" I exclaimed.

"Sorry, not sorry?" was all she said as she gathered her cloak and left me alone again at the edge of the tribe.

PIPER

I was outside the longhouse doing breathing exercises less than an hour after meeting Agnarr at our tree. I was glad I decided to see him before the ceremony. I wanted him to be the first to see the dress. The look on his face was enough to tell me how much he liked it. I couldn't smell his arousal the way he could mine, but I could tell it was costing him everything not to pull the dress off of me. I smiled to myself. *All in good time.* Billie, Odin, and Brandr stood with me, waiting for the sign it was time to enter. I couldn't bring myself to make Odin carry the rings on a weird pillow so he would carry the beautiful box Osif made for my ring open and out in front of him. He took his job very seriously.

The double doors were flung wide and music floated out to where we were huddled. Billie gave me a crushing hug before linking arms with a very confused Brandr and heading toward the doors at a distinctly measured pace. Billie, having been a bridesmaid before, reminded me of the importance of walking slowly. I watched them disappear into the longhouse and then looked down at Odin.

"Are you ready?" I kneeled to his level, so we were eye-to-eye, reminding me of our first meeting. It was only fitting to be here with Odin, the first orc I met.

"I'm ready," he said firmly.

"Okay then, I think it's your turn. Remember. Give the rings to Brandr, then stand next to him."

"I remember. Mom told me to remind you to breathe," he informed me before turning and heading into the longhouse.

I laughed, thinking of Tora telling Odin that I might forget to breathe. And then it was just me, alone, with my thoughts outside the longhouse. Billie told me to count to sixty after Odin left before heading in. I got to sixty, took a couple of steadying breaths, and slowly headed in. I was grateful for the girls who remembered a bouquet for me. I'd thought to decorate the longhouse with winter greenery, but Jo remembered that Billie and I should have bouquets. Mine was a lovely arrangement of greenery sprinkled with small red berries. I purposefully looked at the bouquet as I crossed the threshold of the longhouse, letting everyone get a good look at me before I headed down the aisle.

I took a step, and everyone in the room stood and turned to me. I'd forgotten about that part. I tried to collect my thoughts, but everything seemed to be scattering with all eyes on me.

Breathe in, breathe out. You can't faint in front of the entire tribe. Breathe. Just breathe.

I looked up, and there he was. I locked eyes with Agnarr. He could see the panic in my face. Panic that no one else would recognize. He smiled and nodded to me, silently telling me to keep my eyes on him. That was it. I could do that. I could walk down the aisle and let him hold me up. I smiled back. A genuine smile, not a smile I put on when things weren't okay, but I had to pretend they were. A smile because it was him I got to walk to.

I took a step and then another, and then, before I knew it, I was there. I handed my bouquet to Billie and grabbed Agnarr's open hands, hanging on for dear life. I looked up and smiled, grateful for his steadying presence. I was marrying him. I was ruling this tribe with him.

"Hi," he whispered.

"Hi," I breathed.

"Are you ready?"

"Yes. Definitely," I squeezed his hands in mine.

"Please be seated," Astrid said, addressing the entire tribe. "Are you okay?" she asked quietly as everyone settled.

"I am now." I didn't take my eyes off Agnarr.

"Members of Fýrifírar, we gather on a historic day for our tribe. Today, we recognize the bonds that Agnarr and Piper have made, both human and orkin. We celebrate a newly mated pair, and we announce them as the new leaders of our tribe, welcoming a new bright future for Fýrifírar. Jarl Agnarr and Jarlin Piper will rule, side by side, equal in all ways, Elska mates, husband and wife. They stand here before you to publicly share their commitment to each other and their shared commitment to Fýrifírar. Agnarr, Piper, would you like to exchange vows?"

Agnarr and I nodded, and I was suddenly glad that we'd decided I would go first.

"Agnarr, I've never had anyone to rely on. I built a wall to protect myself because I had no one to protect me. I don't need that wall anymore. You are my safe place to land, my island in a choppy sea. I know I can rely on you in all ways. You see me and you love me, knowing my struggles and my flaws. I give myself to you completely, knowing I am safe in your arms. I'll love you forever," my voice was quivering by the end, but I got there without shedding a tear. I gave Agnarr a shaky smile, nervous that I'd crack open at whatever he'd prepared.

"Piper. I have wanted a mate since I realized how special the bond between my parents was. I'd all but given up hope on finding one when I saw your delicate frame slumped over in my chair. I hadn't even seen your face when I knew. Being in your presence woke up part of me I didn't know was asleep. And when I finally got to meet you, to understand your fiery spirit and your iron will, I knew there would be no one else for me." Agnarr paused and wiped the tears streaming down my cheeks with large thumbs, holding my face in his hands. "I am still learning what it means to have you as a partner, but I know you are all I will ever need. You make me laugh, even when I shouldn't. You show me what I am capable of, pushing me, pushing us to be the best we can be for each other and this tribe. I will be at your side as long as I remain on this plane."

We stood, just staring at each other for a beat. I could hear Billie attempting to hide sniffles behind me, and it pulled me back to reality and the realization that all eyes were on us.

"Members of Fýrifírar, please rise," Astrid called out to the crowd. Every member stood, "Do you, members of Fýrifírar, promise to help guide Jarl Agnarr and Jarlin Piper to informed decisions, to advise and counsel, and to assume the best intentions?" she asked.

"We do," the entire tribe boomed in unison.

"You may be seated. Brandr, the rings, please." Brandr passed Astrid the box. "Piper and Agnarr, are you ready to exchange rings?"

We both nodded. We hadn't practiced what we would say as we placed the rings on each other's fingers. Agnarr took my ring from the box and slid it onto my still-shaking finger, "Piper, this ring is a symbol of our commitment to each other and our commitment to Fýrifírar. I promise to love you for as long as I have breath in my lungs." Damn this hulking orc and how much I loved him. I was not a pretty crier. I probably looked like a fucking mess.

I took Agnarr's ring from the box, seeing it for the first time. It bore the same intricate details as mine, just on a larger scale. I took Agnarr's hand and took a deep breath, "Agnarr, this ring is a symbol of my commitment, love, and devotion to you. I promise to love you and lead by your side for the rest of my days," I slid the ring onto his finger and gripped his hands in mine.

"Agnarr and Piper, do you promise to be faithful to each other in all ways, to rely on each other when times are hard, to wake up every day and choose each other?"

"We do," Agnarr and I said in unison.

"Do you promise to do what is best for Fýrifírar and seek opinions and guidance from others when making decisions for the tribe?"

"We do."

"Agnarr and Piper, you may seal your commitment with a kiss."

Cheers erupted around us but sounded faint as if everything had fallen away. It was only the two of us. Agnarr pulled me into an embrace, his hands warm on the bare skin of my back, his hungry lips on mine. I kissed him back with all that I had as if trying to convey the truth of all the promises I had just made. I was his, wholly and utterly. Knowing I would never have to take a step without his steadying presence was enough to keep me happy from now until forever.

LEXICON

Old Norse is a parent language to many of the Northern Germanic Languages. It is a "dead language" and there is controversy between scholars and historians about the pronunciation and use of many words.

The language used by the orkin is a combination of Old Norse, present day Icelandic, and some proto-Germanic terms. It is not meant to reflect any specific language, history, or people.

While some Old Norse mythology has inspired some aspects of the universe *Abandoned on Niflheim* takes place on, there is little correlation between what I have depicted and any original texts, myths, histories or oral traditions of Old Norse and present day Northern Germanic cultures.

Planets
Niflheim /niv-uh l-heym/ – planet where Piper and other females have been left.
Midgard /mid'gard/ – orkin term for earth.

Tribes

Fýrifírar /fyːri-fiːrar/ – orkin living in the forest of Niflheim.
Vátrfírar /vaːtr-fiːrar/ – orkin living on the coast of Niflheim.
Snaerfírar /stnaiːr-fiːrar/ – orkin living in the snowy region in the highest settlements of the Fjall Mountains.

People and Sayings
Já /yaː/ – yes.
Jarl /yärl/ – chief or earl (masculine).
Jarlin /yärl-in/ – chief or earl (feminine).
Kveoja /kʰvɛðja/ – language spoken on Niflheim.
Elska mate /ˈɛlska/ – fated mate.

Flora and Fauna
Hestr /hest-err/ – beasts for riding and carrying goods, similar to horses. They have 8 legs, short curly hair, and a snout more similar to a cow.
Baldrian /bald-ree-an/ – soothing herb, similar to valerian.
Furutré /ˈfu.ra-treː/ – tree found in Niflheim, similar to pine.
Örn /œrtn/ – a large bird, similar to an eagle, local to the Snaerfírar.
Fjall Mountains /fjatl/ – mountain range down the spine of the continent.
Björn /pjœtn/ – bear.
Skogkatt /skuːgkAt/ – large, long-haired fairy cats who live in the mountains and climb rocks.
Valhnot /vahl-nut/ – tree nut local to Fýrifírar, medium brown in color.
Grautr /græʉt-er/ – grain like porridge served for first meal, usually sweetened with fruit and syrup.
Niflfýri - forest of mist that separates the Fýrifírar from the Snaerfírar.

Time

Dagr /ˈdɑgr̩/ – day.
Vika /ˈvika/ – week.
Mánuthur /ˈmauːnʏðvr/ – month.
Ár /auːr/ – year.
Áratugur /auːr aˈtʰʏːɣvr/ – decade.

ABOUT THE AUTHOR

Jen has been reading for as long as she can remember. She used to get in trouble for reading *Little House on the Prairie* under her desk in elementary school. Jen's day job is advocating for adolescent mental health, something she doesn't see giving up any time soon.

Jen is married to a very polite Englishman she brought back as a souvenir from her college study abroad trip. She has identical twin mutants who make her question her sanity daily. She enjoys reading about alien peens, napping, and watching soothing cooking shows.

She is a goth kid at heart and truly wishes she could wear platform combat boots and black nail polish on all occasions.

* * *

www.authorjeniferwood.com

Made in the USA
Middletown, DE
10 May 2024